FIVE GOLD RINGS

Twelve Days of Christmas

Emily E K Murdoch

DRAGONBLADE PUBLISHING, INC.

ARE YOU SIGNED UP FOR DRAGONBLADE'S BLOG?

You'll get the latest news and information on exclusive giveaways, exclusive excerpts, coming releases, sales, free books, cover reveals and more.

Check out our complete list of authors, too!

No spam, no junk. That's a promise!

Sign Up Here

www.dragonbladepublishing.com

Dearest Reader;

Thank you for your support of a small press. At Dragonblade Publishing, we strive to bring you the highest quality Historical Romance from some of the best authors in the business. Without your support, there is no 'us', so we sincerely hope you adore these stories and find some new favorite authors along the way.

Happy Reading!

CEO, Dragonblade Publishing

Additional Dragonblade books by Author Emily E K Murdoch

Twelve Days of Christmas
Twelve Drummers Drumming
Eleven Pipers Piping
Ten Lords a Leaping
Nine Ladies Dancing
Eight Maids a Milking
Seven Swans a Swimming
Six Geese a Laying
Five Gold Rings
Four Calling Birds

The De Petras Saga
The Misplaced Husband (Book 1)
The Impoverished Dowry (Book 2)
The Contrary Debutante (Book 3)
The Determined Mistress (Book 4)
The Convenient Engagement (Book 5)

The Governess Bureau Series
A Governess of Great Talents (Book 1)
A Governess of Discretion (Book 2)
A Governess of Many Languages (Book 3)
A Governess of Prodigious Skill (Book 4)
A Governess of Unusual Experience (Book 5)
A Governess of Wise Years (Book 6)
A Governess of No Fear (Novella)

Never The Bride Series
Always the Bridesmaid (Book 1)
Always the Chaperone (Book 2)
Always the Courtesan (Book 3)

Always the Best Friend (Book 4)
Always the Wallflower (Book 5)
Always the Bluestocking (Book 6)
Always the Rival (Book 7)
Always the Matchmaker (Book 8)
Always the Widow (Book 9)
Always the Rebel (Book 10)
Always the Mistress (Book 11)
Always the Second Choice (Book 12)
Always the Mistletoe (Novella)
Always the Reverend (Novella)

The Lyon's Den Series
Always the Lyon Tamer

Pirates of Britannia Series
Always the High Seas

De Wolfe Pack: The Series
Whirlwind with a Wolfe

Selina and Arthur and Dorothea
Caroline
Esther
Arabella
Lucy
Sophia
Jemima
London
Rupert and Frances
Joy
Harmony
William and Leonora
Olivia
Isabella
Katarina
Maria
Bath
Chalcroft
Fitzroy

CHAPTER ONE

"AND OF COURSE, when I heard about it, I was completely agog!"

Esther Fitzroy allowed her sister's words to wash over her as they sat in the drawing room of their London home. At least, *her* London home. Caroline had been married near on four years now but took every opportunity to visit and bring them the latest gossip.

As if they could not read the gossip sheets themselves.

"And what do you know, Lady Romeril had absolutely no idea her precious—"

"Caroline, can you not think of anything more interesting to talk about?" Lucy interrupted with a roll of her eyes.

Esther stifled a laugh. *That was always the way with Lucy.* Quick to speak, quick to offend. It would never do, of course, for her to spend more than five minutes thinking about what she was about to say. What was the point?

A book in her lap, which had been ignored for a good hour, Esther sighed happily. There was something about the beginning of December, the crisp of the leaves, the sudden change in their air. The feeling of Christmas to come.

It also brought back two of her married sisters, making the Fitzroy family whole again—save for Arabella, who had decided to spend Christmas with her husband's family. Esther had never noticed it before, and at times had thought the house far too busy with them there; but somehow, Caroline and Jemima's absences made a markable difference.

Not that she would ever own it to Caroline, of course. That was the trouble when one's sister had married an earl.

"Well, I dare say I can find something else to speak on, if the topic truly offends you, Miss Lucy," said Caroline snippily, drawing her head up high and glaring at her younger sister. "But I would have thought you would be interested in learning the latest developments of courtship!"

Esther cut in before Lucy could say something that someone, at the very least, would regret. "What a kind thought, thank you, Caroline."

She caught Lucy's eye and tried not to grin. Well, they had spoken often of their sister Caroline's desire for grandeur—a desire which had never surfaced until poor Stuart had suddenly ascended to the title of the Earl of Cheshire.

It had been rather a shock to the system, from what Esther had seen.

Still. Caroline had slid very easily into the life of a countess, as they had all predicted, and now there was nothing to do but appease her. Most of the time. Her children had stayed in the country with her mother-in-law, and Caroline was distracting herself from the separation from her babes by gossiping.

Lucy had returned to her embroidery, and Esther would have much rather followed her example and returned to her book—but there was a piqued look of upset on Caroline's face she knew they would suffer through the entirety of Advent if she was not appeased.

Esther smiled to herself and took a deep breath. *Well, there was nothing for it.* She had always been the peacekeeper of the family, and it was a role she was happy to perform.

Most of the time.

An entire hour more of Caroline's snide gossip, however, was not the reward she would have typically sought. Ah well.

"Tell me, Caroline," said Esther pleasantly, hoping her sister did not hear the boredom she was doing her best to quash. "When will Stuart be joining us?"

A more natural smile crept across the face of the Countess of Cheshire. "Oh, I hope it will not be too long. He had to stop at his club, of course, make sure his face was still known there—"

"And pay his bills," muttered Lucy out the corner of her mouth, a sly smile on her face.

Caroline resolutely ignored her sister as Mrs. Castle, the housekeeper, came in to light the candles. Though it was just after luncheon the day was dark, gray clouds scuddering across the sky.

"I suppose he has spotted an acquaintance or two there and is so beloved by them that he has been encouraged to sit a while," said Caroline, genuine pride in her voice.

Esther could not help but smile. That was the Caroline she remembered, the one who had loved Dr. Stuart Walsingham not for any riches—for he'd certainly had none—nor a title, which neither of them had known about when he had first engaged her affections.

No, it was the kind heartedness of the doctor which had first attracted her sister, and Esther had to admit herself relieved it had been in that order. She was not sure how she would have felt if Caroline had chased after an earl.

"That is the trouble with Stuart, he is so thoughtful and considerate with his friends," Caroline was saying, and Esther hurried to follow the conversation. "Why, only yesterday he was telling me about the poor Duke of Kendal!"

She raised an eyebrow suggestively, evidently waiting for one of her sisters to ask just why the Duke of Kendal, a gentleman they had never heard of, could be described as "poor."

Esther looked around the room. Lucy was studiously examining her embroidery, refusing to look up, and Sophia was by the window. She evidently had absolutely no interest in their sister's tale.

Talking a deep breath, Esther ensured there was an intrigued look on her face before she said, "Truly, Caroline? What about the poor Duke of Kendal?"

"Well, that is precisely it!" Caroline said triumphantly.

Esther was almost certain she heard a snort from Lucy's direction but did not look round. "What is it?"

Her book had just been getting to an interesting section. It really was too bad she had to pay attention to Caroline's nonsense. How much longer would she be staying? The Cheshires had a remarkably fine house just a few streets away, and though Caroline was a frequent visitor at the Fitzroy home, she did not actually live here. Not anymore.

Just a few more minutes, Esther told herself. Then she could get back to her book.

"The Duke of Kendal has lost his fortune," said Caroline triumphantly.

Esther waited for the rest of the story, but it appeared that was it. "Oh. Poor man. What a shame."

There was a snort from Lucy again, but Esther still refused to look around. *Well, what else was she supposed to say?*

They had never met the Duke of Kendal; until this moment, Esther had never heard of him. There were plenty of fools about the world; it was hardly her concern if one of them decided to part with his fortune.

"You are rather heartless, you know," chastised Caroline with all the superiority of an older sibling. "The poor duke placed all his fortune into a shipping scheme, do not ask me which one, for I forget, on the certainty it would enrichen him—but the ship went down! All hands saved, thank goodness, but all opportunity lost. The man is quite destitute."

Esther nodded, her heart twisting a little. She was not one to crow over another's misfortune, especially when it appeared from Caroline's tale that the man could hardly have known the ship was going to go down.

But then, as their Papa often said, speculation was just that—

speculation. One never knew what was going to come good and what was going to be an unmitigated disaster. It appeared the Duke of Kendal had discovered that himself, at great peril.

"Poor man," came an unexpected voice from the window.

Esther and Caroline turned to see Sophia shaking her head.

"Precisely what I thought," Caroline said, pointing a finger at their sister. "Poor man, I said to Cheshire, the man will have nothing!"

Esther tried not to smile at the way her sister said "Cheshire" so unconsciously. She could well remember a time, years ago now, when the news that Dr. Stuart Walsingham was the new Earl of Cheshire had ended his engagement with Caroline.

The entire Fitzroy family had been convinced that would be it, but here they were. Two children later, and still more in love than ever.

"The man will have to marry well, mark my words," said Lucy, evidently unable to keep away from the conversation any longer. "A great fortune will be required for a duke."

"A fortune like ours, I suppose," teased Esther with a wry smile.

Laughter from all four Fitzroy sisters echoed around the drawing room at that, but Esther had not entirely meant it as a jest.

It was well known, after all, that Arthur Fitzroy, though not the eldest of his brothers, had managed to grow his fortune substantially over the last two years. Each of his unwed daughters now had a substantial fortune, a dowry just waiting for a gentleman to request their hand.

That strange twist in Esther's stomach returned. *Well, it was a strange thought, wasn't it.* That her dowry, just sitting in Papa's bank, could in fact be the fortune a man like the Duke of Kendal needed to restore his name.

Poor man indeed, Esther thought. The elderly man must be disappointed to see his financial hopes sink to the bottom of the ocean, but it was not as though she was going to marry an old codger just for that!

No, she had endured plenty of suitors, misers the lot of them, circling around her in the hope she would immediately bestow a pleasant look...

One of them had even had the audacity to ask her Papa's permission to marry her!

Esther almost laughed at the memory. She had never met the man in question before—she would not consider him a gentleman. A gentleman would have had the good manners to at least converse with her before approaching her father.

No, she was more accustomed to men pursuing her purse.

But the Duke of Kendal would have to find a woman like her, Esther supposed—at least, as wealthy as her but far less discerning. She would not accept an old curmudgeonly man just because he made a poor error of judgment.

"And the thing is," said Caroline, dropping her voice into a conspiratorial whisper as though she was afraid of being overheard—ridiculous, in Esther's mind—"is that the Duke of Kendal—"

"Should my ears be burning?" came the voice of an unknown gentleman.

Esther started. So focused had she been on Caroline's words, she had not noticed the door had opened—revealing her brother-in-law, the Earl of Cheshire, and a handsome young man she did not know.

He was grinning. His strong jaw was made all the more handsome by the expression, something Esther tried not to look at once she noticed it, and he was taller than Stuart by a few inches.

"Ah, Kendal," said Caroline smoothly, as though she had not just been gossiping about his financial affairs to her sisters. "How pleasant to see you."

Esther swallowed. *This was the Duke of Kendal?*

For some reason, she had pictured an old gray man with whiskers, wearing the fashions of her grandparents, sitting in a cold, creaking house he could not afford to heat.

Not this dashing, grinning, handsome man.

"How pleasant to be seen by you," the Duke of Kendal said charmingly as he stepped into the room. "Though I admit, it is even more pleasant to see you situated amongst such lovely ladies. Good afternoon."

He bowed to each of them in turn, and Esther found a strange heat pooling in her chest as his gaze met hers.

Was that a twist of his lips into a mischievous smile as he saw her?

"Ah yes, some of my many sisters-in-law," said Stuart with a laugh as he followed his friend into the room and clasped his hands onto Caroline's shoulders. "Caroline you know, of course, and Miss Esther Fitzroy sits with her book."

Esther inclined her head, unsure precisely whether she should rise and curtsey. He had entered their home and with a member of her family—but he was a duke. She compromised by flushing, which was most irritating. The last thing she needed was for the man to get...*well. Ideas.*

"Miss Sophia sits by the window, and Miss Lucy appears to be embroidering very poorly," said Stuart cheerfully.

Lucy replied by throwing the embroidery at her brother-in-law, which made all of them laugh, save Caroline, of course.

"Lucy! And before the duke, no less!"

"Oh, I am sure the poor duke does not mind," teased Lucy, her face suddenly falling as she realized what she had said.

A discomforting silence fell upon the room as Lucy looked, panicked, at Esther.

Esther sighed. Once again, here she was, acting as peacekeeper. If only her sisters did not always manage to get themselves into scrapes.

"Tell me, Your Grace," she said brightly. "How do you find London this Season?"

For some strange reason, the Duke of Kendal glanced at Stuart, who nodded. Only then did he turn back to Esther and smile brightly.

"Very pleasant, Miss Fitzroy, I must say," he said, moving to sit beside her.

Esther almost shifted back in surprise, not expecting such a close encounter with a gentleman she did not know. And a duke, too.

It was rather inconvenient that he was so handsome. If only she could concentrate and stop looking at his face, his broad shoulders, the way his eyes crinkled when he smiled.

Esther swallowed. This was certainly not the Duke of Kendal she had imagined.

"What are you reading?"

And the worst of it was that no one else seemed to notice, Esther thought wildly. Why, Sophia was looking back out of the window as though something fascinating was occurring, and Lucy had got up to retrieve her embroidery, chatting away happily to Caroline and Stuart.

None of them seemed to realize there was a remarkably handsome duke sitting beside her. *A duke!*

"Miss Fitzroy?"

All she had to do was stay calm, Esther told herself while trying to fold her hands in her lap, getting in a tangle with her book in which a finger had been marking her place. He would be gone before she knew it, surely, and then she could just forget him.

Forget him. Esther's gaze flickered over his face, and her stomach lurched horribly.

As though it would be that easy.

"Miss Fitzroy, are you quite well?"

Esther blinked. The duke had spoken, and she had not being paying attention in the slightest.

"I beg your pardon?" she said hastily, trying not to think how foolish she undoubtedly looked.

But the Duke of Kendal did not appear to notice, or if he did, he did not care. He smiled, pointing at the book in her lap. "Your book. What is it?"

Esther looked down at her book, relieved to have an excuse to look away from him for a moment and try to find her equilibrium, even if it caused a knot to appear in her stomach.

"Book," she said stupidly.

The duke nodded, as though she was not being a complete fool. "Yes, I wondered what it was. Are you enjoying it?"

Esther swallowed and looked up once more into his gray eyes. This was remarkably strange; she had never found herself so tongue tied before. It was not as though he was the most handsome man she had ever seen; that had been a Prussian prince she had once spotted, at a distance, at a ball hosted by Lady Romeril.

At least, she had thought he was a Prussian prince. That was what Jemima, one of her other married sisters, had whispered at the time.

And the Duke of Kendal was not nearly so dashing as all that brass and military finesse. But there was something about him. Something strange. Something none of her sisters appeared to have noticed.

Esther blinked. "What?"

Without saying another word, the Duke of Kendal gently reached over and removed the book from her lap.

The gentlest of brushes of his finger against hers caused heat to flood through Esther's body, and she immediately looked away.

This was ridiculous. She was only embarrassed because she had been told about the duke's unfortunate financial situation just before he had appeared. That was all.

Embarrassment. That was the only thing this fiery heat through her could mean.

"*The Romance of the Forest*," the Duke of Kendal read on the title page. "My word."

"It is actually a very good book," Esther said, not entirely sure why she was defending Mrs. Radcliffe so imperiously. "Have you read any of her works?"

"I have, as a matter of fact."

Esther stared. She had never met a gentleman who had read a

Mrs. Radcliffe—or at least, one who would admit to as much. *Only a novel*, the newspapers called her work. As though novels could not be most excellent.

"I have not read this one, though," he continued. "I am glad to hear you are enjoying it. I shall...erm. Find a copy. Somewhere."

Esther swallowed. It was not her place to mention it, of course. She would never speak of a gentleman's income before him, let alone remark on a person's misfortune.

Even if they were remarkably handsome, as this man was.

But it was rather awkward. The poor man—there it was again, Caroline had managed to get into her mind—obviously could not purchase a copy of *The Romance of the Forest* for himself, if he truly was as penniless as her sister had said.

"You can borrow mine," Esther said without thinking.

The Duke of Kendal's gaze met hers. "I beg your pardon?"

Esther felt the flush move up her chest and to her neck. *Hateful, hateful thing!* That was the trouble with being a redhead.

"I just thought—if you wished to read it, there is no need for you to wait for a copy in the circulatory library," she said in a rush, hoping he would not guess where her thoughts had been wending. "I am almost finished with it."

For a moment, she was certain he would be offended. A mere miss, offering a favor to a duke? Ridiculous.

Yet Esther knew the gentleman had no other choice but to accept. Propriety demanded it, after all, even if his circumstances had been better.

"Thank you," said the duke with a charming smile. "That would be most pleasant. Here."

Fishing a card from his waistcoat pocket, he handed it to Esther, who was very careful not to touch his fingers with her own as she took it. Whatever had occurred when he had taken her book certainly could not happen again.

"Th-Thank you," she said, hating how her voice faltered.

"The pleasure," said the duke in a low voice, "is all mine."

Esther swallowed as she looked up and met his gaze. The way he said that, as though there was a promise within it, not just gratitude. As though he was teasing something to come, something she did not entirely understand.

It was most unaccountable.

What was even more unaccountable was the twisting knot in her stomach that was getting worse and worse the longer they sat here. What did it mean? Why was she so unable to be calm around this gentleman?

"Any snow, Sophia?"

Esther jerked from her reverie as Lucy's question was shouted across the drawing room.

"No, worse luck," said Sophia with a sigh. "Gray clouds, but nothing."

"Still enough light for a walk though," said Stuart in a bracing voice. "Greatcoats and scarves and all that. What say you, Kendal?"

If Esther was not mistaken, an odd look passed between the two gentlemen, one of secret communication she could not decipher.

But then it was gone. She must have dreamt it, she decided. After all, what sort of secret message could her brother-in-law and the Duke of Kendal possibly have with each other?

"Capital idea," said the duke, rising to his feet. "Miss Fitzroy, will you be so good as to accompany us?"

Esther's mouth fell open as his hand appeared before her. *An invitation to walk with a duke.* It was certainly not what she had expected this Christmas.

"Oh yes, we'll all go," said Lucy cheerfully.

"I would rather stay," complained Sophia fitfully, and a debate began between them with Caroline chipping in, as she did.

Esther said nothing. She could not drag her eyes away from the gray ones of the duke as he stood there, hand outstretched, ready to help her stand.

"Well, Miss Fitzroy?" said the duke in a low voice. "Will

you?"

Esther swallowed. Miss Fitzroy. Yes, she supposed she was Miss Fitzroy now, not Miss Esther, as she had been for so much of her life.

Miss Fitzroy. A duke wished to go for a December walk with Miss Fitzroy. Her.

"Yes," she found herself saying, unable to look away. "I will."

CHAPTER TWO

THE DECEMBER AIR was crisp and sharp in Esther's lungs as the gaggle of Fitzroys—and the Duke of Kendal, the gentleman she was attempting to ignore—stepped out onto the pavement.

"Goodness, it's freezing!" shivered Lucy, pulling a woolen scarf closer around her.

Esther smiled at her sister, grateful she had said something, filled the silence. The question was, how long would it be before she was required to say something?

She was not entirely sure she had enough in her mind to speak. So much of it was clouded with the presence of the Duke of Kendal beside her. Esther could feel the impact of his presence even when he was silent.

"Miss Fitzroy, will you be so good as to accompany us?"

Esther shivered but not due to the cold air. What had started as a normal day in December, the hint of Christmas starting to feel more real, was becoming something quite different.

"Well, where to?" asked Caroline with a smile at her husband.

He returned it. "Vauxhall will be pleasant at this time of day, I think, and not too far."

There was general murmured agreement, and even Esther remembered to nod. That was it. Focus on her family. There was nothing more pleasant—well, freezing—than an afternoon walk with her family.

Yes, there was a duke there, too. But she could ignore him.

"Walk with me," Esther said decidedly, turning to Lucy and looping her arm into hers.

There would be no opportunity for her to make a fool of herself before the Duke of Kendal, or accidently let slip that she knew far more about his financial affairs than she had any right to, if she was walking along the pavement with Lucy.

But within a minute of the five of them wandering toward Vauxhall, her sister pulled away.

"Lucy?" Esther said hastily, trying not to hear the panic in her voice.

The Duke of Kendal was right behind them. What if he got the wrong idea—what if he thought Lucy was purposefully removing herself so he could walk with Esther?

"I thought I would call on Percy," said Lucy brightly. "It's quite all right, I'll meet you there. I won't be long."

Panic gripped Esther's heart. With Caroline and Stuart walking arm in arm before them, entirely absorbed in their own conversation, Lucy's absence would leave her alone with...

"Lucy," began Esther. "Wait, I'll come with—"

"I'll see you at Vauxhall!" Lucy shouted over her shoulder.

She had already stepped off the pavement, forced a barouche to halt at great speed, and scampered across the street without a care in the world.

Esther sighed heavily and wished to goodness she had said something. It was not as though she had anything against Percy— or Lord Ardingley, as she supposed they should call him, now they were out in Society—but still. It did leave her in rather a discomforting position.

"I shall have to make up for your sister's absence," came a gentle, teasing voice.

Esther flushed as the Duke of Kendal stepped forward to take Lucy's place, though thankfully he did not offer his arm. That would be the last thing she needed. Caroline would gain absolutely the wrong idea, and she would not be able to live it down.

Their mother certainly would not let her.

"Miss Lucy appeared to be in a great hurry," commented the duke into the silence as the Fitzroy sisters and their companions turned a corner.

Esther could not help it. Though she knew it was utterly bad manners to do in company the instinct was too strong. She rolled her eyes.

A chuckle emanated from the gentleman beside her as they approached the gates to Vauxhall. "Now, Miss Fitzroy, there is a story there, and one I must hear. Why such an expression?"

"Oh, call me Esther," said Esther, discomfort growing in her stomach at each mention of "Miss Fitzroy."

Caroline and Jemima, their half-sister, had been the Miss Fitzroys of the house for so long, it felt strange to be addressed so, even if it was now her due.

For some reason, the Duke of Kendal's eyebrows raised, but he nodded as he said, "Very well, then…Esther."

Scalding heat seared Esther's cheeks as they entered Vauxhall, Caroline chattering away ahead of them.

That had not been entirely what she had meant. She had intended the duke to call her "Miss Esther," rather than the staid and formal "Miss Fitzroy."

But instead…

"Very well, then…Esther."

Esther swallowed. Well, there was nothing for it now. It would be far too rude to retract her permission. She would just have to hope Caroline did not catch a duke speaking to her in such an intimate way.

As a gentleman may do to his lover, for example…

"So, tell me about your sister."

Esther blinked. "I beg your pardon?"

The Duke of Kendal jerked his head back the way they had come. "Miss Lucy. She disappeared off rather rapidly, I thought."

A wry smile appeared on Esther's face, despite herself. "Yes.

Well, she has disappeared off to retrieve a friend of ours—more a friend of hers, I suppose, though we have known Percy all our lives, as far back as I can remember."

"Percy?"

Esther swallowed. She should not be using such intimate terms before a duke; it was scandalous!

Hesitating a moment, she looked around Vauxhall and wondered whether she could distract the Duke of Kendal from the wayward ways of the Fitzroy sisters and onto another topic of conversation instead.

"I did not expect London to be so busy this time of year," she said airily. "Very pleasant."

"And Lucy is a particular friend of this…Percy?"

Esther did not need to be looking at the Duke of Kendal to know what he was supposing, and as she turned to him, she saw a knowing smile that was entirely wrong.

"Oh, it is not like that," she assured him with a laugh. "Goodness, the idea of any of us and Percy—I am sorry, Your Grace, I have not explained."

"Jack."

Esther blanched. It was the cold of the day; it could not be the startling look the Duke of Kendal was giving her.

A look so strange, she had never seen the like of it before. Intense and meaningful and full of something that could have been desire—if anyone had ever looked at her like that.

Which no one had, of course. It was her imagination.

"Jack?"

"It's John, really, but people I care about call me Jack," he said with a lopsided smile.

Esther forced herself to grin. "I am not sure whether I should be calling a duke by his first name."

"You asked me to call you Esther," he pointed out.

Glancing away, Esther saw rather to her chagrin that Caroline and Stuart had walked on. Why, they were practically alone.

Alone in Vauxhall with a penniless duke who had just asked

her to call him Jack.

Esther was almost certain she was dreaming. This was not the sort of thing that happened to a woman like her—though if it did, she realized with a slow smile, it would be because the man saw her and something more than her.

A dowry, for example.

"Well, Jack," Esther said slowly, her tongue stumbling slightly on his name, "Percy—Lord Ardingly, I mean—his father and mine were good friends before he died. We have known Percy forever, he is more a brother to us than anything else. He and Lucy are perhaps the closest."

A strange expression covered the duke's face. "I am sorry to hear of his loss."

Esther stared. Loss? She had not been aware Percy had suffered any loss, at least not recently—and as far as she knew, the duke had never met Percy before.

"Loss?"

"His father."

"Oh. Oh!" Esther smiled at the misunderstanding. It was so easy to do, of course, so many people thought Papa was her father. And in a way, he was. "No, I meant my father."

Jack's eyes widened. "But—but I met your father just now, a few minutes ago—Cheshire introduced me, in your hallway!"

Esther smiled, a little wearily, and saw disappointment flash in his eyes. It was strange; the man was so attuned to her expressions. She would need to be careful or she would start revealing things she did not wish to.

Like just how pleasant it was speaking to him, for example. Why, Esther could not recall being so comfortable in a gentleman's presence in years.

"Caroline and I are full sisters, but Jemima is our step-sister, and the others are half," Esther said succinctly. "It is all rather confusing, and I beg you will not worry yourself about it. I rarely do."

It was easy to speak to flippantly, Esther supposed, for she had plenty of time to be accustomed to it.

Jack, however, looked wretched. "I am sorry."

"Do not be," said Esther with a brisk smile, the winter wind rushing past them. "I do not remember my father, and Papa has been there for us for so long…I cannot recall any other way. I took his name several years ago, though I was born a Forrest and I suppose, technically, I still am."

Jack nodded. "So you are Miss Forrest." He laughed as Esther wrinkled her nose. "Right, right. I shall remember that."

Esther's stomach lurched, but she tried to focus on the path ahead of them. *It was just a kind remark,* she told herself. Just one of the polite little things a gentleman like him would trot out for any young lady they were with.

It was not special for her. He was just being polite. Extremely polite.

"So, Percy is merely a friend of the family?"

"Yes," said Esther, gratefully grasping the neutral conversation as they turned a corner. "Yes, a friend of the family."

Jack nodded and smiled wistfully. "I have never had a friend like that—one which goes back that long, I mean. I would like some, but I suppose it is like anything important. One has to start now to reap the rewards many years later."

Esther swallowed down her instinct—which was to say she would be his friend.

His friend? She was not a chit of fourteen, offering to befriend a sorry looking gentleman. Jack was a duke! A duke, moreover, who likely as not had plenty of friends and acquaintances and was merely being polite.

She glanced at him through her lashes and flushed as she caught his eye. She turned away, focusing once more on the path before them.

Did he think her pretty?

The thought had flashed through her mind before she could stop it, and that despicable knot in her stomach tightened.

Whether the Duke of Kendal thought her pretty was neither here nor there, Esther told herself firmly. She was not here to flirt and make a mockery of herself. He was a friend of her brother-in-law, and that was all.

Absolutely all.

"Keep up you two!" Caroline's shout echoed as she looked back at them.

Did she have to make such an exhibition of themselves? Was it not bad enough that their matching red hair made it impossible for them to go anywhere without people gawping?

"You rolled your eyes again."

Esther looked hastily up at the duke. "I did?"

Jack grinned as he nodded. "You don't even realize you're doing it, do you?"

She shook her head rather guiltily. "Jemima says it is my absolute worst habit, and I have to say I agree."

"Jemima?"

"One of my sisters," said Esther a little wearily. *Why try to make friends, after all, with five sisters to keep you company?* "The step-sister, she married a Captain Rotherham near four years ago."

Jack nodded. "It must be pleasant, being part of such a large family."

"It must be, I suppose," said Esther without thinking, then laughed wryly as she saw Jack's expression. "Well, you know how it is. Only children long for siblings, those burdened with more siblings than one wish for solitude…"

"I suppose it often goes that way," agreed Jack. "But now it must be different, is it not? With some of them married?"

Esther swallowed before replying. It was remarkable, really, just how quickly a conversation in the Season could drift toward matrimony.

Not that the Duke of Kendal had any ideas on that, surely?

"Jemima and Hugh will be back for Christmas, and the Cheshires are here for the Season," she said quietly. "And my other married sister, Arabella, is visiting our family in Bath with her husband—oops!"

A stray stone had caught her heel, and Esther, never one for paying attention to where she was going, tripped, arms flailing as she rushed to the ground.

And then halted.

Strong hands encircled her wrists, halting her sudden downward fall, and Esther's stomach lurched as she saw Jack holding her carefully.

There they stood, Esther almost in his arms, her heart racing as she attempted not to look into his eyes, failing completely. He was actually might be the most handsome man she had ever seen.

"Careful," breathed Jack, not looking away. "Here. Take my arm."

It was all Esther could do not to fall again, her legs giving way at the attentive way he carefully folded her hand onto his arm.

She was arm in arm with the Duke of Kendal. *The Duke of Kendal!*

This was ridiculous. She certainly should not be doing something so scandalous as accept the attentions of a gentleman who was absolutely penniless.

"I am glad your family is coming together for Christmas," said Jack, starting to walk forward as though nothing had happened.

Esther did her best to keep up with him, still not entirely sure how her legs were moving. "Yes. Most of us."

"Of course, your sister in Bath," said Jack with a nod, as though it was outrageous he had forgotten so quickly. "Do you find…"

Esther did her best, she really did. She knew she should listen, knew it was incumbent upon her to be entertained. But it was difficult when feeling the strength and warmth of Jack's arm under her hand, to think at all, let alone listen.

The Duke of Kendal. If she had seen him dancing at Almack's, he certainly would have done something strange to her stomach, making her heart flutter. Just to look at him was to admire him.

But this was something quite different. Why, she could not recall ever having walked arm in arm with Percy Ardingley, for goodness' sake, a gentleman who was almost a brother!

Yet here she was. Looking to all the world as though she was being courted by the charming man.

Wasn't she?

The thought flickered through Esther's mind. Was this what it was to be courted? Most gentlemen she knew were interested in pursuing her purse, her dowry the only thing of interest to them.

"Esther?"

Esther flushed at the intimacy of hearing her name on his mouth. "Yes, I am sorry. I was listening."

Jack raised an eyebrow. "Were you?"

There was such a teasing grin on his face that she could not help but laugh. "Well, no. Not really. But that is no reflection of your conversational skills, I assure you, Your Grace."

"I thought I asked you to call me Jack," he said softly.

Esther shivered. There was something about the way he looked at her, the way the world melted into the background and all sounds started to fade. How attentive he was. How charming. How intriguing. How…poor.

"Why, only yesterday he was telling me about the poor Duke of Kendal!"

Esther looked away hurriedly from the gentleman who was smiling so prettily at her. Of course, how could she have forgotten?

The Duke of Kendal, while rich in charm, was entirely lacking where, to most, it counted—in the pocket.

It was hardly possible for a gentleman to live the life a duke was expected to live—lavish, luxurious, and best of all, liberal to his friends—with not a penny to his name.

Esther's heart sank. So, he was interested in her dowry, then. Just like the rest of them. Though she had hoped that he would be different, there was not much between them.

He wished to consider getting his hands on her dowry.

Only then did a flicker of memory enter her mind: the way Stuart had encouraged Jack with a nod toward her direction.

The knot which had started to grow the moment the Duke of Kendal entered the Fitzroy home twisted once more.

Was it possible…had Stuart perhaps suggested the duke could find a willing bride in the Fitzroy family? Impressive dowries they all had, but she as the eldest was perhaps considered the most likely to accept the attentions of a poverty-stricken duke.

"Esther? Are you quite well?"

Esther started and looked up into the gray, stormy eyes of the Duke of Kendal. "Yes. Yes, quite well."

Jack beamed. "Marvelous, because I wanted to ask…well. I hope it is not too much of an imposition, but I so would like to…"

Esther saw that Caroline and Stuart were waiting for them at the gate. Their walk, it appeared, was over.

"Yes?" she said, unable to prevent herself smiling at the gentleman upon whose strong arm she was leaning.

It was wonderful, being so close to such a man. His mere presence had an effect on her, one Esther could not deny. It was rather like when she had one too many glasses of sherry.

Heady. Giddy. Tingling all over her body.

"I was wondering if you would like to go on another walk?" said Jack in a rush.

Esther frowned. "Now?"

"No, not now—any time, I suppose, except now," Jack said, slight color appearing in his cheeks. "Tomorrow, perhaps. The day after. Whenever is most convenient for you."

Halting on the path, Esther removed her hand from his arm. Well, she had not expected it of him, but then she supposed a duke had to find a fortune somewhere, and where better than in the purse of a pretty woman?

True, he was only interested in her dowry…but an odd and rather rebellious thought struck Esther as she looked into Jack's eyes.

Yes, he only wished for her money...at the moment. But what if she could make him fall in love with her?

What if, in fact, she could seduce him—*not seduce him*, Esther thought hastily, *not entirely*—more encourage him to the point where he truly cared for her? Make it a love match, not merely a merging of a title and a fortune?

"Well?" asked Jack a little nervously.

Esther beamed. *Well, it could hardly hurt to try, would it?* "I would be delighted, Your Grace."

CHAPTER THREE

"WHERE ON EARTH have you been?"

Esther flushed as she reached the top of the stairs, Lucy and Sophia gawking from the doorways of their bedchambers.

"I have not been gone that long," she said defensively just as the dinner gong sounded below.

She looked hastily at her sisters. They were dressed for dinner, their elegant silk gowns contrasting with the slightly damp hem of her own cotton muslin.

Well, it was not as though she had purposefully stayed out longer than she had intended. This was her third walk with the Duke of Kendal, the first which they had gone on alone, though they had kept to the streets of London so no scandalous remarks could be made.

Esther smiled. She was starting to long for those walks, those moments the two of them had to talk.

True, it was dark, which should have been the first sign that Jack's conversation was far more diverting than she had expected—but it could not be that late, could it?

"It's dark!" Lucy said with a giggle. "'Tis almost time for dinner—Papa was starting to talk about sending out a search party!"

Esther flushed. That was the trouble with curious sisters.

They were wont to notice things, ask questions, demand something as bold as the truth.

Why could she not just do what she wanted without people asking precisely what—

"Where have you been?" asked Sophia quietly.

Esther swallowed. She was not one for lying; she never had been. None of the Fitzroy sisters had ever been liars, and as far as she knew, neither were their numerous cousins.

But in this moment, staring into the eyes of her sisters, she was tempted to.

The truth was so much more interesting, of course, which was why she wished to keep it to herself. None of the family needed to know she had spent all afternoon walking with Jack.

Walking, talking, laughing. Hearing his ridiculous stories about escapades on the Continent—half of them exaggerations, Esther was sure—and in turn spilling some secrets of her own. Stories of Caroline and Stuart mostly, and her sister Jemima, but still.

Esther had hardly noticed the darkness creeping around them, the lamps being lit as they approached her home. The company had been too good.

The gong downstairs rang again.

"Lord, dinner must be ready," said Lucy, hastily tying on a necklace with a blue ribbon that clashed gloriously with her hair. "You had better get changed quickly, Esther, or Mama will wonder what on earth has happened to you."

The thought of being questioned by the Fitzroy matriarch was enough to force Esther from her stupor and toward her own bedchamber.

"Tell them I'll be down in a minute!" she called out behind her.

"Caroline and Stuart are already here," Sophia shouted after her. "Don't be too long!"

It was a good thing, Esther told herself, that her heart was thumping so wildly already from the mere presence of Jack, as it spurred her onward, and she was able to extricate herself from her muslin gown quickly. It was a little tricky to do get into her silk one, the buttons on her back, but years of practice after sharing a maid with three sisters—Jemima and Caroline had one between them—meant Esther was only slightly late and slightly ruffled when she came downstairs.

"I do apologize for being late," she called out with a beaming smile as she scampered down the stairs, across the hall, and toward the dining room. "I was out late walking with…the Duke of Kendal."

Esther blinked. *It was not possible.* She was dreaming, so lost in her thoughts of the walk she had enjoyed with Jack earlier that afternoon that she was seeing things.

But, apparently, she was not the only one. Her Papa, Arthur Fitzroy, clapped Jack on the back and smiled at his daughter as he stood near the head of the table.

"I have just been saying to young Kendal, Esther, that he simply must join us for dinner. Poor man hasn't eaten yet, can you imagine?"

Esther smiled weakly as all the eyes of her family turned to her. *Yes, she could well imagine.* In the last week she had spent more than a little time with the penniless duke, and at no point had she ever seen him eat anything.

The poor man must be starving.

"And I said I simply couldn't," said Jack cheerfully, as though he could not be happier to be there. "And so it was decided I would stay for dinner, though I am not entirely sure how it happened."

Esther had to smile. There was no one like her parents for making people feel welcome, and of all people to bring to the table, there was no one she wished to see more than Jack.

Not that she should own such a thing, of course. Not even to herself. The gentleman was supposed to be falling in love with her, not the other way around.

"How pleasant for us all," she said delicately, and looked

around the room to see which seats were taken.

There was her mother, Selina, looking magnificent at the foot of the table. On either side of her were Caroline and her husband, and beside Stuart, Lucy. That left two seats beside Caroline, and one by Lucy.

Esther's heart skipped a beat most painfully. To sit beside Jack at the dinner table…why, it would be marvelous. The chance to really impress him, although precisely how she was not sure yet.

It turned out it was far more difficult to make a gentleman fall in love with you than she had considered.

"Here, sit down by your father Sophia," called their Mama. "Beside Lucy, there you go."

She would be seated by Jack.

"You look all flushed, Esther."

Esther started and tried to smile at her sister. "Nonsense, Lucy, I am just tired, that's all."

"And well you might be, gallivanting out at all hours, we have hardly seen you this December!" said their Papa happily as he indicated to Jack that he should be seated and took out the chair at the head of the table. "Where have you been going, that's what I want to know!"

"Just…" Esther swallowed as she sat down beside Jack, determinedly not catching his eye, but unable to prevent her chest from tightening, her lungs battling for every breath.

"Just?"

Esther tried to smile at her father and wished heartily he would not ask such questions. "Just getting fresh air, Papa."

"Not that we need much more, I am sure it will snow soon," said Jack, placing his napkin on his lap. "Here, let me."

Before Esther could say anything, the duke had picked up her napkin and placed it delicately on her lap, his fingertips brushing her thighs through the material.

And then it was over. Esther had gasped, hoping no one had noticed, but certain they had. How could they not notice such a scandalous thing!

But as Jack leaned back in his seat, his face was calm, though there was a smile dancing across his cheeks.

Heat warmed her cheeks, and Esther looked hurriedly down at her plate. What did the man think he was playing at? Another touch like that and the whole family would assume they were…well.

Involved.

Engaged to be married.

Something worse. Or better. Esther was not entirely sure, but it was certainly entirely impossible. She should have begged a headache, gone upstairs, and refused to sit here, next to him.

Though it was rather pleasant. Seated here, with Jack beside her, Esther found her body slowly relaxing as the conversation meandered around her, sometimes just one, sometimes splitting into two and filling the room with sound.

Jack joined in quite pleasantly, as though he had always been there. As though he was precisely where he ought to—

Esther gasped, a noise thankfully hidden under the chatter of the table. Something absolutely extraordinary had happened; Jack's hand was on her thigh under the table. Not just touching. Moving. Stroking.

She swallowed. She should not think such things of course. It was rather scandalous, but she could not help it.

Jack, the Duke of Kendal, was gently stroking her with his fingers, moving inexplicably to her inner thigh.

Delight skimmed across her body, radiating from her leg to the rest of her body as Esther tried to concentrate on what she was supposed to be doing—eating her dinner. But how could she?

Looking up, Esther's eye caught Jack's, and he grinned, winking again.

No one else would have caught it.

What did the man think he was doing?

"You are not exactly dressed for dinner, I must say," said Stuart with a teasing air. "I suppose we shall have to take that as proof that you did not loiter here in the hopes of an invitation."

The family laughed, and Jack laughed with them—though how he was able to do so, with his fingers now sliding gently up and down her inner thigh, Esther did not know.

"Yes, I am afraid I am rather shabbily dressed for such an elegant table," Jack said ruefully, as though his fingers were not sparking pleasure Esther had never known.

Esther attempted not to glare at the gentleman who had tempted her out of doors almost every day that week, even in a light snow shower which disappeared almost before it had begun.

The dratted man knew all too well, and the worst of it all was that she could do nothing to stop his fingers, teasing and stroking, making her whole body quiver…

Well, perhaps this scandalous touching would help him to fall in love with her. He certainly seemed to be enjoying himself.

The conversation continued, but Esther could pay it no heed, not with Jack's fingers doing the most incredible thing to her body—and it was all she could do not to gasp as one of his fingers trailed gently over her secret place, right between her legs.

Oh, the pleasure…it was more than she had ever known. How could such a gentle touch create something so…

"Jack," Esther breathed.

A smile twisted his lips. "You like it?"

His breathed words were heard only by her, and Esther could do nothing but nod as his fingers returned to her secret place, stroking again, causing sparks to fly through her body, sparks she wanted more of.

"Jack…"

She glanced at him, cheeks flushed, and he gently removed his hand from her as though nothing had happened. Esther sagged against her chair, hardly able to breathe. What on earth had he been thinking—and why did she wish for him to continue?

"—time for Christmas," Caroline was saying to her mother most imperiously. "I suppose she will be here?"

"Of course Jemima will be here, and darling Hugh as well, I trust," said Selina placidly. "They always are, and they will be this year."

"What about you, Kendal?" asked Arthur.

Esther's eyes flickered to Jack. It was rather strange, her father being so cavalier with his guest's official formality, but then, did she not call him Jack?

"I will be spending Christmas here," said Jack. "I mean—not here, of course."

The table roared with laughter—everyone except Esther, who flushed and looked back down at her plate. *Goodness, she would have to concentrate*; almost everyone else had finished with their roast chicken and vegetables. The gravy was starting to drown the peas on her plate.

"In London, I mean, rather than the country," Jack said with a rueful smile. "I find the manor rather too large to—I mean, I would not want the trouble of hosting Christmas. Far more pleasant in town."

Caroline, Sophia, and Lucy all looked away, cheeks flushed.

Esther knew precisely what had embarrassed them. The briefest mention, that was all, but it was perfectly clear to everyone at the table that the Duke of Kendal was not able to heat his country home.

Sympathy for the man, utterly unable to keep himself warm due to a simple error, poured through her. It was simply unfair that such a man, of such high honor and estate, should be reduced to such circumstances.

Her dowry, large as it was, would certainly make a difference there.

The thought caused her stomach to twist, and Esther glanced up quickly at Jack before looking down at her meal again. To think, he could perhaps return to elegant Society if they married.

He would have her riches, the ability to entertain and dine with the very best. And she...she would be a duchess. It was a startling idea, one that had not occurred to her, despite all her determination to make him fall in love with her.

A duchess. Duchess of Kendal. Esther had never been one for grandeur, but even she could admit that the idea made her heart flutter.

But best of all, she would be married to Jack. She would be his wife, and he, the handsome, charming, rather witty man she had spent the last week getting to know, would be her husband.

"Well, I think we ladies shall retire."

Esther jerked her head up. Her mother was rising elegantly from her seat, and Caroline had already followed suit.

"Retire?" she said instinctively.

Leave the table, now? Leave Jack, whom she was finding to be the best company in the world? Who was able to make her feel…feel everything? Feel things she had never even known were possible?

Leave him?

"Come on, Esther."

Esther started and saw she alone of the ladies was still seated at the dining table, food untouched.

Her mother was smiling. "Come along."

For an instant, one Esther thought would last forever, she considered asking her father if she could stay, if she could break all rules of decorum and remain with the gentlemen as they drank port and smoked cigars.

But Esther rose, red cheeked at the mere thought of her rebellion.

She was not that sort of lady, no matter what Jack's fingers threatened to do to her.

The drawing room felt cold and dull after the excitement of the dining room—after the stroking sensuality produced by Jack's fingers, Esther reminded herself, cheeks hot as she sat as far from the fire as possible.

Lucy picked up her embroidery with a heavy sigh, Sophia took her favorite place by the window—this time looking into the room, as the dark night was obscured by curtains—and Caroline and their mother sat by the fire.

"I have just received a letter from your Uncle William," said Selina impressively. "And I must say, I am disheartened to hear what he has to say."

Caroline leaned forward eagerly. "Tell us, Mama. Does he write of that terrible slander about them in the newspapers? I could hardly believe it when I saw it, the outrage!"

Their conversation continued, but Esther could not take heed of their words, interesting as the topic was.

"You like it?"

Not after what she had just experienced.

Esther's fingers curled in her lap, unconsciously starting to mirror what Jack had done to her but managing to stop herself just in time. The idea that such delicate strokes could cause such sensations…it had never occurred to her.

It would be all she could do to prevent herself from repeating such an exercise.

Heat blossomed through her chest, a strange sort of throbbing centering between her legs. *Just what did Jack think he was doing to her?*

"Ah, here they are," said Sophia eagerly. "Papa, come and sit by me. I was thinking…"

Esther's head jerked up, her hands moving to her sides as though she had been caught. The gentlemen had indeed appeared, far sooner than she had expected.

Their Papa obediently went to the windowsill, and Stuart, as expected, moved to sit beside his wife. Esther smiled. Even after their second child had arrived, there was no keeping them apart. That was a real love match. Rare, for someone of his standing.

Esther could barely lift her eyes to see Jack, but as it turned out, it did not matter.

The gentleman sat beside her, a wry smile on his face. "It's been hell without you."

She had to smile at that. "I bet you say that to all the ladies."

"Only when it's true."

Esther's shoulders slumped. *Well, she should have expected that.* He was a duke, after all. Had he not had plenty of opportunities to tease and delight the ladies of the *ton?*

"And therefore," Jack continued in a low voice so only she heard him, "so far, only to yourself."

Esther breathed a laugh. "You do tease me rotten, Jack."

"I know," he breathed. "And I would like to do a great deal more to you."

A flush overcame Esther's face at the sound of such scandalous words. *Did he know…surely he must know what was suggested in those tones?*

"Well, we should at least attempt to be civil," she managed to say. "What would you like to talk about?"

"Anything from your lips will be music from heaven."

Esther laughed to hide a myriad of confused emotions. How was it possible for a gentleman to entirely unsteady her? Just when she thought she had a level footing in the conversation, Jack was ready to unseat her.

Topple her. Tup her even, perhaps.

"Don't speak such rot," she breathed.

When she was able to bring herself to look at him, Esther saw Jack's gaze focused on her lips, the lips he had just spoken of, and she colored further. This man was not shy about his desire for her, that was certain.

The question was, would he be so reticent in his intentions?

"I…I was sad to hear you will spend Christmas alone," said Esther, scrabbling for something to say that would not lead to more indecent behavior. "You…you should spend it here. With us."

Where precisely the words had come from, she was not sure—except the idea of anyone, let alone a handsome, winsome duke spending Christmas Day alone was abhorrent.

And the idea of spending such an intimate day with the Duke of Kendal was delicious.

Jack's eyes were wide, and for the first time that day, she had him on the back foot. "Spend it with—you cannot just invite me to your Christmas Day celebrations?"

"Why not?" challenged Esther in a gentle voice, a smile creeping across her face. "There is always room here, and I would...I would like you to."

As their eyes met, a rush of excitement flooded Esther's body. Oh, she wanted more than Jack to spend Christmas with them, but she did not have the words to ask for what she wanted—and even if she did, she certainly would not say them.

Not here before her family!

"You would like me to?"

Esther nodded, her throat somehow dry, words impossible.

Jack hesitated, then rose to his feet. "I must go."

"Must you?" Esther rose hastily, heart thumping painfully, wretched at the thought of him leaving. Had she been too forward? Suggested something utterly impossible? Why was he leaving?

"Oh, what a shame," said Stuart lightly. "Esther will see you out, won't you, Esther?"

Esther frowned at her brother-in-law, wondering why he thought it appropriate to order her about in her own home, but smiled at Jack. "Of course."

The hall was dark, lit only by the light spilling out from the now empty drawing room. Esther felt a little awkward as she watched Jack pull on his greatcoat, desperate to say something, but not entirely sure what.

"Well," she said helplessly. "I suppose we will see each other—Jack!"

His name was hissed, barely a breath, as Esther fell against the wall, the duke pushed up against her, his lips on her neck and his fingers curled around her secret place.

Esther shuddered as his touch returned, the touch she had longed for the moment it had been removed, and this time she was ready for him, knowing what she wanted, knowing the pleasure he could give her.

"Jack," she breathed, her eyelashes fluttering as tingles of hedonistic pleasure rippled through her body, his fingers teasing and rubbing a rhythm of hot delight between her legs.

Her hands had reached for his shoulders, holding him close, Jack's other hand on her waist holding her upright, for which she was grateful.

"But—but someone will see," Esther breathed, the scandalous nature of their encounter somehow heightened by the risk they took.

"No one will," murmured Jack as he grazed her collarbone with kisses. "Anyway, doesn't that make it rather exciting?"

Esther was going to reply that of course it did not, but her words stuck in her throat. Firstly, because they would be a lie, and secondly, because Jack's frantic rhythm had now moved deeper, deeper between her legs, and she could not bear it. The pleasure he was creating was sparking sensations she had never known before, and she ached, ached for him, ached for more, and something was happening, something that was overtaking her—

"Jack," Esther whimpered.

Perhaps he knew just how desperate she was for him, how close she was—whatever it was, Jack's mouth left her neck and crushed her lips, and Esther's body shuddered as a crest of pleasure overcame her.

Oh, it was too much, too much! Esther closed her eyes, losing herself in the moment, forgetting her family, the fact they were in the hall, everything. All she could concentrate on, all she could feel, was Jack.

Eventually the pleasure rippled away, subsiding gently, though her body still felt wonderful, as though she had been dipped in warm honey. Jack ended the kiss and broke apart from her, breathing heavily. His gray eyes did not for one instant look away from hers.

"I will see you soon," he said in a jagged voice, stepping suddenly away and slamming the door behind him.

Esther slid slowly to sit on the floor, her whole body sensitive after such delight. What on earth was she going to do?

CHAPTER FOUR

THE CHRISTMAS MARKET was absolutely heaving.

Esther should have guessed as much; it was December, the turn of the tide when holly and ivy became fashionable, when ribbons of gold and silver were sought after, when the most perfect gift for one's loved ones was impossible to track down.

"Pies! Get your pies, hot and hearty!"

"Mulled wine, mulled wine, one for you, one for your lady!"

"Trinkets and jewels, rings and brooches, all you'll need for Christmas!"

Esther breathed in the heady atmosphere of the market. It appeared every year, seeming to spring up from the ground as though it was just waiting there, out of sight, excited for opportunities to sell wares.

The...the moment between them, Esther was not entirely sure what the correct wording was for such a thing, had happened. It was impossible to deny.

He had touched her. Jack. He had touched her in a way that had swept pleasure through her, her entire body tingling, pushed her to an edge that Esther had never believed possible.

Cinnamon, ginger, spiced ale, and mouthwatering pies lent their scents to the air.

The market was a delight to the senses, with colors clashing wonderfully from stall to stall. It was the most exciting place to be in the lead up to Christmas, and Esther always ensured to visit with one or more of her sisters to find unique and unusual gifts for each other.

But not this year.

Esther's hand curled around her reticule, hanging carefully from her left hand. As usual it contained what her mother considered the absolute essentials; about three shillings in coin for emergencies—though what emergency would only require three shillings, Esther could not tell—along with a ten-pound note from her allowance, a handkerchief, a pencil, and several copies of her mother's card.

Just in case, her Mama always said with a wink. In case you meet a nice young gentleman and wish to make his mother's acquaintance.

But unusually, today her reticule also contained something else. Something scandalous. Something Esther could never have imagined she would receive.

A letter.

A note, really. Esther was not sure whether it could be called a letter if it was only eight words long, but still. She had received correspondence from a gentleman—a gentleman to whom she was not related.

It was the sort of behavior, in her Mama's words, young ladies should not permit.

But she had. And when the note had been brought to her last evening by a servant, well after the last post, Esther had been astonished to see an ornate K on the seal. Her astonishment had been nothing to her excitement when she opened it, however.

Esther

The Christmas market. Tomorrow at midday.

Kendal

Short though the missive was, it was absolutely clear. The Duke of Kendal—Jack, if she could be bold enough to say it again in his presence after what he had done to her—wished to see her.

Esther shivered as a freezing breeze whistled past, the noise of the Christmas market almost overpowering. She had been careful to arrive at five minutes to midday. Lucy may tease her about punctuality, but she was not going to miss him.

But he was not here. At least, she could not see him. What felt like hundreds of people were milling about the place, moving from stall to stall, bartering with some and scoffing at others, baskets or bundles weighed down as they went…

But no Jack.

Esther swallowed. It was not a trick. She was almost certain; none of her sisters would be so cruel as to do such a thing.

Well. Maybe Jemima. But as she was not yet in London, it seemed unlikely she had gone to such trouble to fabricate such a thing from a distance.

Yet, why else would he not be here?

Esther's fingers closed around her reticule, as though she could feel the presence of Jack's note within it. He had been bold to send her such a thing. So why go to all the trouble of sending her such a thing if he had not intended to actually—

"Esther."

Several people looked around, herself included, and they were treated to the view of a gentleman dressed in a fashionable greatcoat, piping along the sleeves in the military style, and a top hat that seemed to tower over the crowd.

And a smile that made her knees weak.

Esther stared, rather astonished as Jack pushed his way through the crowd, her heart lurching as she became conscious of all the eyes watching her.

Watching him. Watching that handsome man shout out her name—*her first name!*—then push his way toward her.

It was impossible to know what they were thinking, and from what Esther could see, none of them knew her…but still. Gossip was always alive in the streets and drawing rooms of London, and she was certain it would not be long before Lady Romeril had a little word with her mother about the scandalous goings on she was getting up to…

"There you are," said Jack a little breathlessly as he reached her. "I've been waiting for…I mean…you are right on time."

Heat pooled in Esther's stomach at his words, the intensity of his look. It should be illegal to look at a lady like that, and in public. Though foregoing it was something she was not entirely sure she could live with.

A gentleman looking like that at her…and this gentleman in particular…it was doing strange things to her legs that Esther could not quite understand. They were quivering, ever so slightly. Most unaccountable.

Thankfully, her skirts hid the worst of her frailty, and Esther managed to smile. "I do apologize, Your Grace, I was not entirely sure where in the market to meet—"

"Jack."

Esther stammered as the Duke of Kendal gently rebuked her. "I-I beg your pardon?"

"I thought we had agreed, you were Esther, and I was Jack," said the duke lightly. "It is…important to me."

Esther swallowed.

Well, this was not the plan at all. She had decided, had she not, to make the Duke of Kendal fall in love with her? He sought her purse, and she sought his heart. It was that simple.

It did not feel that simple any longer. Not after what they had shared but a few days ago. Why, as she looked up into the gray sparkling eyes of a duke—*a duke!*—it was only now starting to dawn on her that if she was not careful in guarding her heart, Esther would be very much in danger of falling in love.

Which absolutely would not do.

Transforming her nervous smile into a bracing one, she said, "Well, thank you for coming."

"Thank you for accepting my invitation," said Jack softly as he stepped closer. "Thank you."

He had only stepped closer, Esther told herself, because of the crush of the market. *He wanted to ensure I heard him. There could be no other reason. The man had not fallen in love with her already...had he?*

No, it would not be that simple. Which meant she had much more to do before she could claim to have won the Duke of Kendal's heart.

"How could I say no?" Esther said. "How could I decline spending time with you?"

Though she had spoken the words to be provocative, to spark a reaction in the duke, Esther found to her chagrin that it sparked a reaction in herself, too. It was true. The truth of it spread through her body, creating a strange sort of tingling along her fingertips.

Jack's eyes blazed with a strange emotion she did not recognize, then settled once again into their normal stormy gray. "Well, then. Shall we?"

Indicating with his hand, she thought for a moment that he was going to offer his arm—but he did not. Disappointment stirred in her stomach most strangely, and Esther attempted to push it aside. She was the one attempting to convince him that he was in love with her, that was her plan. One she should not forget.

"The Christmas market is renowned," Jack said conversationally as they approached the first stand, "for its extravagant and diverse stalls. Have you been here before?"

"Been here before?" repeated Esther with a laugh. "You are not a true Londoner unless you have been here every year, Jack. Tell me, have *you* been here before?"

Jack smiled wryly. "Only the once. I suppose that does not make me a true Londoner?"

"I suppose not," said Esther, pointing at two pies and handing over a sixpence. She placed one of the steaming hot pies in the hands of a surprised Jack. "Here, tell me what you think of this."

"I cannot allow you to pay for—"

"Just try it," Esther said firmly.

For a moment, she was not sure whether the Duke of Kendal was going to obey her. Only then did it strike her that she had just ordered one of the nobility to eat a street pie.

He did, however, gingerly lift the pie to his mouth. Pastry flaked over his cuffs as he took a bite, his expression of confusion and hesitation transforming into one of intense pleasure.

"Oh my—"

"The best pies in London," grinned Esther, nodding at the stall owner and starting to slowly walk forward. "We look forward to them every year."

"I can see why."

They meandered for a few minutes in companionable silence, their pies disappearing. What was it Jack had said?

"I cannot allow you to pay for—"

There, evidence what Caroline had said about the duke had been true.

Not that she had necessarily disbelieved her sister; it was just that stories from the eldest of the Fitzroy sisters had been known to be exaggerated. Sometimes.

But Esther had seen the look of panic on Jack's face; he had no coin, potentially nothing at all on him. It was a bold idea indeed then, to suggest their meeting at a Christmas market. Unless…

Unless that was the point. The thought settled uneasily in Esther's stomach, but she could not ignore it. Unless he was testing the truth of her dowry, her riches. Seeing whether she would spread her largesse for his benefit.

Well, so what if he were? Esther hardened herself to the practicalities of their situation. He wished to court her for her coin, and she wished to seduce him—*not like that*—for his title.

One of them would fall in love, Esther was certain. The question was, which one?

"You will have to come back here again," said Esther as she brushed the final crumbs of her pie from her pelisse. It was impossible to eat the thing politely. "You should bring your family…your brothers, sisters…"

She glanced over at the duke by her side.

"Perhaps," he said, his gaze not meeting her own.

"I suppose it is quite a journey from Kendal," Esther persisted, trying to inject a teasing air into her voice. "Just for a Christmas market."

Jack nodded but said nothing as they reached the end of this particular row of stalls and turned left to meander down another.

Esther swallowed. This flirting lark was rather difficult when one's partner did not appear as interested. It was most infuriating.

She had never been a flirt—in fact, had guarded against it most carefully. Of all their sisters, it was perhaps Lucy or Sophia who came the closest to that description, but none of the Fitzroys could truly be described as flirtatious.

For the first time, Esther wondered whether this was a disadvantage.

"And what about your family?" Jack said. "Do you and your sisters visit here often?"

"Not as often as we used to, I suppose," Esther said wistfully as she tried not to look at the handsome man beside her. *It would not do to get distracted, after all.* "Before Jemima and Caroline were married, we used to come here almost every day in December."

"And now?"

"Lucy and I attend, though often accompanied by Percy."

"And you do not like a gentleman's company?"

Esther glanced over at Jack, who was smiling and felt a twinge of warmth in her gut. *Goodness, he's handsome.* Every inch of him perfectly chiseled by a master craftsman, as though the world had been waiting for a delightful gentleman and so had one made to order.

She swallowed. Why did her body persist in responding so to him when he looked at her like that? It was not as though they could…well.

"I don't mind a gentleman's company in the slightest," she said. "If the right gentleman."

A shove from behind her pushed Esther toward Jack most alarmingly, and he put his hands out to grasp hers, preventing her from falling straight into him.

Into his arms.

"Careful," Jack said softly. "That is the second time you have almost leapt into my arms, Esther."

Esther opened her mouth to speak but could not think of a single thing to say.

"If I were any other man," Jack breathed, no greater volume necessary, they were so close in the heaving crowd, "I would say you were trying to seduce me."

Esther's heart was racing, and that odd ache was growing in her stomach—and not from hunger, or at least not for pies. Something that made her need him, need his touch, the warmth of his hands on hers.

This was far more than she could have imagined, and she had permitted her imagination to run wild last night as she dwelled on his note…

"If I were any other lady," Esther breathed, "I would say you were seducing me."

How long they stood there, her hands in his, their bodies so close she could feel his warmth, Esther did not know. It was impossible to tell. Time had, it appeared, slowed; or the rest of the crowd at the market had disappeared.

And then Jack released her hands and stepped back in one fluid motion. "Well. Shall we…shall we continue looking at the stalls? I am sure you have a few more gifts to buy."

Esther blinked, trying to find her balance. She had never been so close to a gentleman before, except for Jack's will and tempestuous strokes she had welcomed just a few days before. Nothing untoward had happened to her like that before.

But it had now. Something very untoward, though she could not explain it.

"Esther?"

"Yes," she said hastily, smiling and stepping alongside Jack who was approaching some stalls. "Yes, gifts. In fact, I have not purchased any Christmas gifts this year."

Jack raised an eyebrow. "You have much to do, then. Perhaps this stall could offer you choice for all your sisters?"

Esther smiled, then suddenly realized he was indicating the stall before them, and hurriedly turned to look at it. The last thing she wanted to do was make a fool of herself.

She was the one supposed to be enticing him!

Jack had stopped at a jewelry stall, run by a woman with more shawls than teeth, though that was not saying very much.

The woman gave a gummy smile. "Buyin' a gift for y'sweetheart?"

Esther flushed, trying simultaneously to look and not to look at Jack. *Did he color as well?* Or was that merely the rosy glow created by a bitter winter wind?

"Is there anything here you like?"

Esther swallowed. Was Jack asking her whether she wanted a gift for herself or her sisters? It was impossible to tell, and she certainly was not going to ask. No, it was safer to presume the safer meaning.

"I have five sisters, so that means five gifts," she said aloud, highly conscious of how close she was standing to Jack. "It would be much easier if all the gifts were the same, it saves squabbling. You know how sisters are."

Jack smiled but said nothing. Whether that meant he had sisters of his own or he understood her meaning, Esther was not sure.

"What about these, then?" he said lightly, indicating a case of golden rings, each with different stones or more likely, colored glass. "They would look more elegant on your hand."

Had the wind died down? Was that why she suddenly felt warmer?

Esther tried not to think about the way Jack, the Duke of Kendal, had spoken of gold rings on her fingers. Did he understand what that meant, to what he hinted? Had he any comprehension of how close he was to proposing matrimony with such words?

"Five gold rings," she said, her voice slightly strangled. "Well, they are very pretty. How much are they?"

"A pound each," said the woman with a toothless grin. "Or four pounds for five, for the pretty lady."

"Four pounds!" Jack looked outraged. "Four whole pounds for—"

"A fair price," interrupted Esther with a smile. *Here it was, her opportunity to demonstrate her wealth—and her beneficence.* "I shall take five gold rings."

The duke looked astonished. "You cannot seriously be buying four—"

"My allowance and dowry are more than enough for such trifles," said Esther in an undertone, smiling at the look on his face.

Yes, he had sought her out for her dowry, she could see that now. The gentle flush of his cheeks, the way his gaze shifted away from her, the tension in his body.

Jack had considered her a potential bride merely for the coin she could bring to the marriage…but had that changed? Was it possible to change, when she did not know precisely how to flirt with a gentleman of his standing?

"There y'are, miss."

Esther turned to accept the five gold rings in a brown paper bag, which did not bode well—and gave the woman her due, slipping the rings into her reticule.

"Well, you now have most of your gifts," said Jack, "and I must own, Esther, I have need to return to my home in the next half an hour. I have creditors—friends, I mean, who I am meeting there."

Esther flushed on his behalf. There it was again, the accidental evidence of poverty.

Well, that did not mean she had to cease her campaign here. "Do you have time to walk me home?"

She could see the hesitation in his eyes, the uncertainty, the unknown…and yet…

"Of course," said Jack with a broad smile. "Here."

He offered out his arm, and only as Esther took it did she realize just how much she wished to touch him. There was something remarkably comforting about being on the arm of a man like Jack. The only difficulty was how close her home was.

"Here we are," Esther said regretfully.

What had she been thinking? She should have attempted to meander around a longer route, take all the time with him that she could muster…but it was no use. They were here.

"Home again, home again," said Jack with a wry smile. "I should have suggested a longer route. Anything to spend a little more time with you."

Joy soared in Esther's heart as she turned to him. "You thought so, too?"

Her cheeks burned with embarrassment at revealing her own thoughts, but that seemed only to endear her to Jack.

"Oh, Esther," he said in a low voice.

Before she could say anything in reply, before she could do anything, Esther found herself crushed up against her front door—in broad daylight!—with the Duke of Kendal's lips on hers.

The kiss was intense, passionate, his lips caressing hers, his hands on her waist holding her in place, his tongue teasing along her mouth as though desperate for a way in.

Esther's entire body rose in excitement, in joy, in hunger, that ache in her stomach flaring into something darker and deeper— and then it was over.

Jack had stood back, as though nothing had happened.

"Wh-What…" Esther swallowed, heart pounding wildly, unsure whether she would ever be able to speak again. "What was that for?"

Jack swallowed, and she saw the same uncertainty in her heart mirrored on his face. "Because…damnit, I wanted to."

With that, he strode away, leaving Esther to recover her breath and her heart on her doorstep.

CHAPTER FIVE

"ESTHER, PLEASE WOULD you pass me the ribbon?"

Esther stared across the dining table, absolutely covered in festoons of brown paper, gold and silver ribbons, sprigs of holly, and little name cards, and saw not a single whit.

Her vision was seeing something entirely different; at least, it was seeing what she had felt yesterday. What she had never known she could feel. What had felt like the absolute desire of a man and a woman brought together in ways she could never have predicted.

"Wh-What...What was that for?"

"Because...damnit, I wanted to."

Esther shivered. It was unconscionable that she had permitted such a thing to occur, of course, and that was before she remembered the delightful way he had stroked her to ecstasy she had never known before...and never would again. Probably. It was outrageous that Jack had done such a thing to her and right here in her parents' home, too!

No. No, it could never happen again.

A quiver of pleasure, a memory from that moment, crept through her, and Esther swallowed, mouth suddenly dry.

Her eyelashes fluttered slightly as she remembered herself back into that moment. The hardness of the wall behind her, the softness of Jack's lips on her neck, the way his fingers had moved…

"Esther? The ribbon?"

And the trouble was, and Esther was never going to admit this to a single person, was that though she knew she should feel shame for having let Jack kiss her in broad daylight…

She could not. It did not feel wrong. It did not even feel as though it was something she should hide, though she had not mentioned a word of it to any of her family.

But Jack had not appeared ashamed of what he had done, and Esther had enjoyed it too much to feel guilty. The only question was, how was she ever to exist for the rest of her life without sharing such kisses with Jack again?

"Because…damnit, I wanted to."

"Esther? Esther!"

Esther started. "You do not have to shout at me, Lucy!"

Her sister raised astonished eyebrows. "It appears I do, seeing as you have been astutely ignoring me for the past five minutes!"

Esther looked around guiltily. The dining table was covered with countless boxes, not yet wrapped, and she had entirely been lost in her thoughts, not paying heed to their task. These Christmas gifts would not wrap themselves, and it appeared Lucy had done little to solve the problem without her.

A sharp sliver of guilt crept into Esther's heart. She should attempt to pay attention. The last thing she wanted to do was rouse suspicion.

Rouse other things. Arouse Jack.

Esther swallowed and tried to push the thought away. She should certainly not be permitting Jack any greater space in her mind that he was enjoying already.

"I am sorry," she said meekly. "What was it you wanted?"

"Oh, do not worry yourself, I shall get it myself," said Lucy with a laugh. She did not appear affronted, and even smiled after getting up to retrieve the ribbon from the other side of the table. "What's got into you, Esther? Your mind seems to be…elsewhere."

"Nothing has got into me," said Esther, dropping her gaze to the present for her Mama, which she had not wrapped.

Not yet, she wanted to say, then quashed the thought immediately. She was wanton, yes, she had behaved like a harlot, enjoying Jack's touch—but she was not about to give herself over to the Duke of Kendal!

At least, not probably.

She needed to concentrate on wrapping presents.

"I am just a little tired, that is all," she heard herself say to her sister.

It was a pretty mediocre excuse, at least to her ears, but it appeared Lucy was not interested enough to press further. Perhaps her sister had other things on her mind?

Besides, it was not as though she could confide in Lucy. Though she was probably the sister Esther was closest to, after Caroline—and there was absolutely no possibility of sharing this information with Caroline, who would swiftly pass it on to her husband. Esther had no doubt—Lucy was not one to understand these sort of things.

Esther flushed as she dropped her gaze to her Mama's present again, a pair of gloves she had knitted herself.

She and Lucy had shared but few conversations about gentlemen and matrimony, and they had not shed any light on Lucy's preference. Indeed, Lucy had never before, as far as Esther was aware, expressed any preference for a gentleman in their acquaintance.

Which, now Esther came to think about it, was odd. She was of age, after all, and had had a few Seasons in Society.

Had Lucy just never met a gentleman who met her specific requirements?

Esther swallowed. Had she? Yes, she had daydreamed about a husband when younger and had been disappointed in the gentlemen she had encountered as she had entered Society.

None of them compared to the dashing and witty Duke of Kendal.

But he was a duke—and more, he was, as far as she could tell, still entirely fixed on her dowry. Was it possible that he was starting to care for her?

Or, and the thought made Esther's heart sink, was it more likely that the Duke of Kendal had seduced and bedded plenty of ladies before her, and was merely using those selfsame tricks to convince her into matrimony?

"Esther!"

Esther dropped her mother's gift to the floor at Lucy's shout. "Goodness, what?"

Lucy shook her head. "I have been attempting to get your attention for nigh on a full minute. Are you sure you are feeling well?"

Now her sister came to mention it, Esther was feeling a little strange, but she would lay money on the cause being little to do with illness, and more to do with the heady pleasure she had experienced with Jack.

"Lucy," said Esther quietly, retrieving her mother's gloves from the floor, "have you ever…well. Kissed a gentleman?"

Lucy's eyes widened. "What?"

"I am just curious," Esther said hastily, attempting to sound nonchalant. "One hears such stories…"

She allowed her voice to trail away, hoping her sister would pick up the conversation, and she was not disappointed.

"One does indeed," said Lucy with a smile. "Why, I actually saw Miss Tilbury just the other week! She was dressed so fine, Esther, you cannot imagine, and I heard she has taken not one, but two gentlemen as her lovers!"

Esther nodded, pulling a ream of brown paper toward her and trying to fold it around the gloves as her mind whirled. "Yes, yes, good."

"Good?"

"I mean," she corrected quickly, "good of you to tell me. But if a gentleman kissed you, Lucy…what would you do?"

It took all her willpower not to look up, not to show her sister just how intrigued she was. Learning what Lucy would do if she had been kissed by a gentleman could go some way into helping her decide precisely what Jack meant by it all.

And he had done far more than kiss her...

"I do not think a proper gentleman would kiss me, unless he asked permission to do so."

Esther glanced up. Lucy had crinkled up her nose in mild disgust at the idea of a gentleman taking such a liberty—as well she might. Esther would have done the same, before this December.

Before she knew just how delicious it was to be kissed by a gentleman. A gentleman like Jack.

"Percy once said it was only rebellious girls who kissed gentlemen they had no intention of marrying," Lucy continued conversationally. "He was so funny, actually—we were talking about—"

"Yes, well," said Esther quickly. The last thing she wanted was to hear Percy's opinion on the matter; a gentleman would certainly not look kindly on her antics. "But what do *you* think? If a gentleman kissed you, would you think he had serious intentions? Marriage, I mean?"

She did all she could not to hold her breath. Could that be what Jack meant? Was he starting to fall in love with her? Surely, as he had met her father, dined here even, Jack could not consider doing anything that...that delightful, if he did not mean to end it with a proposal?

Lucy giggled. "Percy kissed me once, do you remember?"

Esther's heart sank. It appeared they would not be able to get through the conversation without another story about Percy.

"Yes, he leaned forward most unexpectedly this summer, do you recall, at the fair we attended?" Lucy laughed again. "My word, I did chortle at the time, and he laughed, too, and said what a marvelous jest it was. Do you remember?"

Esther did not remember, but she nodded all the same. So it was possible for a kiss between a lady and a gentleman—

admittedly a man like Percy, which did not count—which was not intended as a precursor for matrimony.

But why should she care? Esther tried to remind herself she was the one trying to entrap the Duke of Kendal into falling in love with her. She was not supposed to be falling in love with him.

"—and when I asked Percy later precisely what he meant by such a thing," Lucy continued, clearly not needing input from her sister, "he laughed away quite merrily and said I was not to take such things to heart, and I must say I have not thought of it since then."

Esther nodded glumly. Well might Percy say that; he was the brother the Fitzroy sisters had never had.

Lucy was continuously bringing up Percy at the moment, Esther was starting to get quite sick of the sound of his name. Which was most unfair to Percy. He had done naught wrong.

It was odd. They had all befriended the lonely boy years ago now, when they were children, but though he was the same age as Caroline, years older than Lucy, it had been the two of them who had truly maintained the friendship into adulthood.

Very strange.

"But why do you ask?" said Lucy suddenly, and Esther saw to her dismay that her sister had a serious frown on her face. "All this about kissing—have…have you…"

The question went unfinished, but it did not need to be. Esther's face burned, crimson likely staining her cheeks, and Lucy's mouth fell open.

"It was just one kiss," Esther said hastily.

It was not entirely a lie. She tried to justify it within herself, telling herself that Jack had only kissed her once…at least, only as a kiss.

The kisses which had trailed down her neck, sparking pleasure wherever his lips met her skin, tantalizingly teasing, as his fingers brought her to ecstasy surely did not count.

"Who?" demanded Lucy, present wrapping entirely forgotten. "Goodness, Esther, no wonder you have been so distracted all day—in all haste, tell me who!"

"It is just...a gentleman," said Esther uneasily.

She was not entirely sure why she did not reveal Jack's name to her sister. Lucy was trustworthy, would not tell a soul any secret she imparted, she was sure of that...

Yet she kept the Duke of Kendal's name to herself.

Perhaps she feared her sister would scream it aloud, alerting the family. Perhaps she thought her sister would get overly excited about the idea of her sister wedding a duke, for that was surely what she would think.

Or perhaps it was something else. Esther could not explain it, but she wanted in this moment to keep it to herself. Keep him to herself.

"A gentleman?"

Esther nodded. "He is...well, I believe he is interested in marrying me for my fortune."

All the excitement drained out of Lucy's face. "Oh."

"But then I thought, if I could make him care for me, truly care for me, then it would be as though it were a love match, do you see?" Esther said eagerly. "And I thought for a while he was starting to care for me...at least, he kissed me, and is that not half of the battle? For he would not have kissed me if he did not care for me, if he were not considering..."

Esther's voice trailed away. Lucy's eyes had glazed over, and she had turned once more to the table, finishing off an extravagant bow on the parcel she had just finished wrapping.

She was not listening. Her sister, to whom she was pouring out her heart, was not listening.

Esther sighed. "And though the entire trick was supposed to make him fall in love with me, I am afraid...I am starting to think I am falling in love with him."

Lucy nodded vaguely. "Good. That's good."

Perhaps Arabella would understand. She was a quiet soul, and Esther knew she felt things deeply. She was the only other Fitzroy sister who might help. She should write to her.

Jemima certainly wouldn't be any help. Esther smiled, despite herself, at the idea of informing Jemima just what she had done with Jack. She would be beside herself!

"Lucy," Esther said firmly. "Lucy!"

Now it was her turn to be ignored. Lucy's eyes were completely glazed over, as though she was thinking of something absolutely vital but entirely different from where they were.

"Just a joke, he said," she said vaguely. "And yet…when I look back—"

"There you two are!"

Both Esther and Lucy quickly scrabbled about to hide the unwrapped Christmas gifts.

"Papa!" Esther exclaimed, half outraged, half laughing as their father hastily put a hand over his eyes in the doorway. "You know you were not supposed to come in here!"

"I forgot, a terrible crime!" said their Papa with a laugh. "I only came to deliver the post, good ladies, please do not poke my eyes out!"

Lucy rolled her eyes as she giggled, getting up and pulling the letter from her father's hand. "You really are very silly, Papa."

"Undoubtedly so," said Arthur cheerfully. "I shall leave you to it, ladies."

He shut the door behind him, and Esther could not help but giggle at how ridiculous he was. There was something so endearing about him.

"It's for you," said Lucy, her face dropping as she sat back at the table. "I thought it might have been from—"

"Percy," Esther chimed in, grinning at her sister's astonished expression. "What, you think I could not guess that?"

Lucy handed over the letter with a sigh, then returned to her wrapping.

The letter was indeed addressed to her, and in a hand that was familiar, though Esther could not place it. It was only when she turned it over and saw the seal that her mouth fell open.

A letter. A letter, sent through the post, to her…from Jack.

There it was, the *K* seal she remembered from the short note he had sent. It was unthinkable that he was writing to her. They were not engaged to be married. They had no understanding. What did the Duke of Kendal think he was playing at?

"Who's it from?"

Esther looked up hastily. "No one," she said automatically, and then cringing at the stupidity of her remark, she lied, "Arabella."

Lucy sighed. "Of course, she would write to you. Tell me about it later, I am going to attempt this ribbon."

Her attention absorbed by the wrapping, Esther felt safe to break the seal and open the letter. Her eyes scanned the first few lines, her mouth fell open, and a dull ache appeared between her legs.

She stood up so hastily her chair fell over. "I will read it upstairs."

Lucy stared at her sister as Esther walked around the table, the letter clutched to her chest. "Esther, are you feeling—"

The rest of the question was broken off by the shutting of the dining room door behind her, and Esther raced up the stairs, heart pounding. There was absolutely no chance she could read that letter with her sister just…just sitting there!

As she closed her bedchamber door behind her, Esther swallowed and sat on her bed.

She must have mistaken it. She could not have read his handwriting correctly. It was possible she had entirely overreacted.

Breathing heavily, Esther smoothed out the letter and started to read once more, her body tingling with every line. She had not been mistaken.

Esther,

I cannot stop thinking about you—about the taste of you, the feel of you under my fingertips. Though I try to sleep, I cannot stop thinking of you, your face preventing me from resting, my entire body aching for you.

You are beautiful. You are magnificent.

And if I had more time, more privacy, there is plenty more I would have wished to do to you, share with you, that would make the pleasure I have given you nothing in comparison.

I crave you, my fingertips crave your touch. Every inch of your skin must be touched by me, every crevice of your body worshipped. When I kiss you, I sense your passion, just under the surface, and it drives me wild that I cannot unlock it.

Not yet.

When next I kiss you, and there will be a next time, that I promise, I will not be so tame, and you will not be so clothed.

I want to know the taste of you, the ache of you, to drive you wild with desire and teasing kisses down your body.

And I will. In time.

Until then, I remain your—
Jack

Esther's heart was beating so hard, she could not think what to do with herself. Such words, such lines, such ideas…

Such actions.

Jack wanted to do them all, and to her. With her.

The dull ache between her legs had grown now, grown into a desperate need. Esther allowed the letter to fall as her eyelashes fluttered, and her hand moved lower, and lower.

She knew precisely what was needed to bring this ache to fruition.

CHAPTER SIX

THERE WERE FAR too many people in London, Esther was sure. It was strange—sometimes she felt it was wonderful that so many people wanted to come here, to her home city, because of its wonders and delights.

But it was on days such as this she raged against the hordes of people crowding the pavements, getting in the way of carriages, making it entirely impossible for a local such as herself to make it down one street without halting. *It was infuriating.*

"Excuse me," Esther said loudly to the gaggle of portly gentlemen who had decided the pavement was the perfect place to stop and have a debate.

A few turned to glance at her, laden with parcels, but none of them moved.

"Excuse me," said Esther, more loudly. "I think you will find you are in the way!"

It was ridiculous! Could they not go to a gentleman's club, or a coffeehouse—anywhere that was not right before her, blocking her path?

One of the gentlemen, probably a little older than her father, wagged his finger. "Quiet girl, the grown-ups are talking."

Esther bristled. She may not have the sparky, fiery temper of her sister Jemima, but that did not mean she could not speak her mind.

"If you do not get out of my way, I shall force you to," said Esther icily, drawing herself up to her full height, such that it was. "And it will go hard with you, I am afraid."

If she had hoped for respectful apologies and her way cleared, she was very much disappointed. As it was, the gentlemen nearest her guffawed, the others asking what they were laughing about.

"This here girl," said the one who had wagged his finger, "had the audacity to...ah. Good afternoon, Your Grace."

Esther stared. *What on earth did he mean, Your Grace?* He was hardly likely to mistake her for a duchess, was he? She was not dressed like one, wearing her mother's borrowed pelisse, which had seen better days after Lucy so unceremoniously took her own.

A hand, gentle yet strong rested on her shoulder. Esther looked up into the smiling face of the Duke of Kendal.

"Gentlemen," he said pleasantly. "I believe the lady threatened you."

They scattered. Faster than Esther could have imagined, without so much as a bye your leave or apology to her, the gentlemen who had proven to be impossible melted away.

"There you are," said Jack quietly.

Esther swallowed. *Did he mean the path he had cleared for her...or had he been looking for her?*

Oh please, looking for her, her heart pleaded.

Which was ridiculous. After receiving his rather inflammatory letter—one which Esther had carefully hidden under a loose floorboard in her bedchamber, for fear that one of the maids may read it—she had heard nothing from him for two days.

Two long days.

Esther had been unsure what to do next every minute of those two days.

Firstly, she could write back to Jack. A letter of her own. A letter describing all the things she would do to him, the things she wished him to do to her. She had even attempted it, once, before shameful embarrassment overcame her. She had burned the attempt.

Secondly, she could wait for him to call. It was surely only a matter of time, she told herself, before Jack came to call on her father and request her hand in marriage. Was it not?

Yet apparently not. Esther had seen nothing of him until this moment, and her relief at seeing Jack was accompanied in equal measure by scandalized embarrassment for looking into the eyes of a gentleman who had written…well.

Such things to her.

I want to know the taste of you, the ache of you, to drive you wild with desire and teasing kisses down your body.

Esther swallowed, her heart racing, and the Christmas bundles she had picked up from all over town suddenly heavy in her arms.

"Jack," she said foolishly.

Jack smiled. "I have missed you, Esther."

Esther nodded, not trusting her voice to speak. What could she say. Thank you for writing me such a pleasing letter? A letter so pleasing it drove me to distraction, drove me to…to pleasure myself?

No, it was too much. She could feel her face boiling.

"You are—are Christmas shopping?" she managed.

There, a nice neutral topic. There was absolutely nothing rakish Jack could say about that, was there?

Jack winked. "Well, I certainly wasn't out here meandering around, hoping to run into you. That would be scandalous."

Esther laughed weakly. Yes, that would be scandalous—but not half so scandalous as the things she had imagined since she received his letter. A whole world of pleasure was opening up to her, one she had not even realized existed, and now all she could do was attempt not to fall into it.

"Well, we would not wish to do anything scandalous, would we?" Esther breathed.

Jack's hand was still on her arm, still clasping her to him. And anyone could see. Anyone walking down Oxford Street would see them, see her and the Duke of Kendal, standing so close together it was impossible to think they had not…

He released her, stepping back. Esther hated it, wanted him back, wished he was still close to her. Which was ridiculous. *She should not be seeking to lose her reputation in such a public manner!*

"I have but one thing to collect," Esther said, hoping to wend her mind back to mundane things. "Will you accompany me?"

It was an innocent request after all, she told herself. She was in public; there was nothing he could do to her…no, after giving it much thought, there was probably not anything he could do to her in public.

Probably.

Jack beamed. "I would be delighted."

It was only a minute down the street to reach her final destination, and when Mr. Rivers saw how laden she was with parcels, he shook his head.

"Miss Fitzroy, you never plan these things!"

"I never do, Mr. Rivers," Esther said ruefully to the haberdasher. "I do not suppose one of your boys could drop all these off at my home? For a shilling, of course."

Mr. Rivers's eyebrows rose. Esther knew it was a prodigious amount for merely delivering parcels, but then, they had not all been purchased at Rivers's Haberdashery, and she would be loath to offend.

"I believe one could," said Mr. Rivers magnanimously. "Here, hand them over."

It was a great relief to rid herself of the parcels—both Sophia and her mother had requested she pick up a few things for them, and Esther's short journey into town had become quite the escapade.

Arms finally free, Esther found Jack remarkably close to her.

"What was it you were going to purchase here, then?"

"Oh, a few things," Esther said airily.

Well, she could hardly say "a replacement ribbon for my stays," could she?

"There is much variety, I must say," said the Duke of Kendal. "I suppose the question should be, what will you leave behind?"

Esther laughed as the haberdasher's eyes widened. "Do not give Mr. Rivers ideas, Jack!"

She had playfully tapped his arm, just as she would do any of her family, but the familiarity took her by surprise—and from the look on Jack's face, she was not the only one.

Esther allowed her hand to fall to her side and tried not to think of just what that arm had done. Holding her up against the hallway wall, keeping her steady as his fingers—

"Well, what will it be?" Jack said, picking up a set of gold bossed buttons and a blue ribbon. "One of everything?"

Esther shook her head as she laughed. "No, I do not think so. You are not going to buy anything for yourself—ribbons for servants, or a pretty brooch for a sister?"

She could have kicked herself the moment the words were out of her mouth. What was she thinking? Did she not know perfectly well the Duke of Kendal was penniless, unable to heat his own country estate? What did she think she was doing, pointing out the man's own poverty, in public?

Esther watched Jack's face fall, discomfort creep into his eyes, and wished to goodness she had thought to keep her mouth shut.

"Yes, I think that will be all I require," she said hastily, taking the blue ribbon.

Mr. Rivers looked disappointed as she took it to the counter. "And…and is that all?"

"All for today," Esther tried to smile. The last thing she wanted to do was upset their haberdasher—he was remarkably quick at sourcing the little bits and bobs they needed. It would not do to make an enemy of him. "You know myself or one of my sisters will be back soon, Mr. Rivers, we can never stay away."

Slightly mollified, the man added her order to the delivery, a shilling and tuppence was handed over, and Esther turned to the man who really mattered.

Jack was standing awkwardly in the center of the haberdashers, looking a little lost.

"Come on," said Esther bracingly.

Without invitation, quite as naturally as she would take the arm of someone she had known for decades, she slipped her hand into the crook of his arm.

Jack smiled. "Where to?"

"I don't know," Esther said. "I do not think it entirely matters, as long as I am…I mean. If we are together."

His gray eyes calmed, the storm disappearing. "In that case, we are quite of the same mind," said Jack quietly.

When they stepped out onto the street, Esther was hit with a blaze of noise—music, shouts, and screams, children rushing forward and almost knocking into them.

"Goodness, what is going on?"

Jack craned his neck. "A musical band, as far as I can see, with a dancing dog. Would you like to have a look?"

Esther shook her head. Animal lover as she was, it hurt her heart to see such animals cruelly used. "Come, let us away in the other direction."

It was like walking against the tide, but eventually they were out of the crush and rush to see the musicians, and the street returned to almost its normal quietness.

Esther took in a deep breath and reveled in this moment. The sun was shining—which meant it was not too cold—and she was arm in arm with the Duke of Kendal. A gentleman who made her feel…

She swallowed. *Everything.*

It seemed odd to continue walking without any reference to the letter, though she was not sure how to begin such a conversation. But it needed to be done. Perhaps he thought she had not received it. Maybe he thought she had been disgusted by it.

"Jack," Esther said quietly.

He squeezed her arm by way of response, which did nothing to quieten her nerves.

"Jack, I…I received your letter."

Jack glanced at her. "You did?"

There it was, the anxious look she expected. "I…I wanted to thank you."

Her words seemed somehow inadequate to describe just how glorious it was to receive such a love letter, for there was no other way to describe it. A love letter, from a duke. A scandalously delicious love letter, one the gossips would certainly love to get their hands on.

She shivered. It was a good thing indeed that she had hidden it.

"And…and you were not offended?" Jack's voice was jagged, his breathing difficult.

Esther smiled, hoping to show him just how little she was offended. "Offended? Oh, no. No. If anything, Jack…the opposite."

Jack stopped dead. Esther jerked forward, unexpecting the sudden change of pace, and was startled to find the Duke of Kendal staring at her as though a woman possessed.

"The opposite?"

His words were breathed rather than spoken. Esther nodded.

It happened in an instant. Before Esther could say anything, do anything, realize precisely what was happening, Jack had grabbed one of her hands in his and pulled her suddenly to the left.

For a heart-stopping moment, Esther could not understand it—he was pulling her directly into a wall!

But she had not spotted the small gap that led to an alleyway. It was dark, the two buildings close together, the quiet noise of the street utterly silent now they had stepped away from it.

And there was something else close, too. Something broad, strong, smelling of masculine power and desire.

Esther gasped as Jack placed his hands on her cheeks, cupping her face to his, but before their lips met, she had already wrapped her hands around his neck. She wanted him, wanted him closer. Wanted to be far closer than was even possible here in this alleyway.

Esther moaned as the kiss began. Teasing and delicate at first, then growing quickly in desire and depth, his tongue begging entrance.

And she let him. There was little Jack could ask for now that Esther would not give him, she knew that.

"Esther," moaned Jack.

She did not know how to respond other than to give him more of what he wanted. Nervously at first, then emboldened by the shivers of desire working their way down her spine as his tongue teased pleasure from her mouth, Esther gave herself up to the kiss.

In fact, her desire was so strong, she stepped forward, desperate to be closer to him, to feel the pressure of his chest against her breasts.

Jack broke the kiss with a breathless laugh as his back touched the alley wall. "Damn, Esther, you know what you want."

Esther could barely breathe, could barely think, only feel. "I want you."

Jack growled as he pulled her closer, one hand on her waist but the other questing forward, managing to capture her breast through her gown as they clung to each other.

It was too much—too wonderful. Esther moaned slightly as Jack's fingers stroked and squeezed, somehow finding her nipple under her pelisse and through her gown. His thumb and forefinger encircled it, causing sparks of aching heat to rocket down her body, building the ache between her legs.

An ache she knew now all too well.

"I want more," Esther murmured between frantic kisses. "More, Jack, more…"

Her words galvanized the duke, his kiss deepening, worshiping her mouth, and something strange and hard was pressing into Esther's hip.

She knew precisely what that was.

Hardly able to believe she was about to do it, she did not

hesitate. One of her hands left Jack's neck and moved down, until a fingertip grazed the bugle of his manhood.

As though he had been burned, Jack pushed her away, breathing heavily in the silence of the alley.

Esther swallowed, her mouth dry, her heart frantically beating, she knew only the Duke of Kendal could finish overcoming her mind.

"Jack…I am sorry—"

"Please do not apologize," said Jack with a dry laugh. "Dear God, the idea that you of all people would say sorry…no, the fault is all mine."

Esther's heart twisted. *The fault.* He did not enjoy it then, thought it was wrong.

Swallowing hard, she tried to keep her voice level. "You regret what we—"

"Regret? Never," Jack cut across her, his searching gaze finally finding hers. Esther was calmed by the mingled look of affection and desire on his face. "No, it is I who should apologize. I had intended…well, let us say a more traditional courtship."

"Traditional courtship?"

Jack's lopsided smile was rather wry. "Flowers and walks in the park with your mother as chaperone, that sort of thing. But I cannot do that with you, Esther. Not now that I know the taste of you. Not now that I know how you quiver under my touch when I bring you to climax."

Esther shivered. It was impossible a gentleman should say such a thing to her—yet he was saying it, and she wanted him to keep saying it.

To—how did he put it? Bring her to climax.

Oh, she wanted to feel that heady pleasure again, and again, to give as well as receive.

But these were wild thoughts, wanton thoughts. Thoughts she should certainly not be thinking.

Besides, Jack had said plenty on pleasure, but little on love. When was he going to consider her more than a purse, more than someone who could just go to a Christmas market and spend pounds on golden rings?

When was he going to fall in love with her?

"A traditional courtship," she repeated. "Something like…like attending the opera together, for example?"

Esther had spoken with a smile, hoping he would leap at the chance to spend a little more time with her.

Jack's face fell. "The opera? Ah. Yes. Perhaps."

Only then did her mind catch up with her desire to be in a dark, warm space with the Duke of Kendal. Of course, how could she have been so foolish; a man in his position was hardly able to afford one ticket in the cheap seats, let alone two seats in the gods?

"My treat, of course, seeing as it was my suggestion," said Esther gently, as though she offered to pay for opera tickets for gentlemen all the time.

Jack's expression softened. "Well, I could certainly see the positive in being with you in the dark. I may even hold your…hand."

Esther quivered at the delicate suggestion of just what he could do with his hands in the darkness and privacy of a box. *Oh, that he would do such a thing…*

She could not help it—and more, she did not want to. Led only by her desire, Esther stepped forward, and for the first time, initiated a kiss between them.

Jack pulled her into a tight embrace immediately, his arms wrapped around her, his lips welcoming the intense intimacy.

It was several seconds later—or perhaps an hour, Esther was not exactly paying attention—when he groaned and pushed her away.

"Damnit, Esther, we could probably do with a chaperone."

"What? Now?" Esther stared, uncomprehending.

"At the opera," Jack said with a laugh. "I certainly would not wish anyone to see what we have been sharing here."

Try as she might, Esther could not entirely calm her heart,

but she managed to lessen in the intensity in her chest by taking a few deep breathes. *A chaperone.* Well, it would probably reduce the likelihood of Jack touching her, bringing her—*what was it?*—bringing her to climax with his fingers.

But perhaps that was all to the good. She could not keep permitting him to make love to her until he was actually in love with her.

"Do not worry," she said with a dry laugh. "I have the perfect idea."

CHAPTER SEVEN

"I NEVER SAID I wanted to go in the first place, and I think it is absolutely ridiculous that you are making me!"

Esther took a deep breath and forced a smile as she looked across the drawing room at her sister.

Lucy scowled. "And there is no use looking at me like that, I will not take my words back nor apologize. You could have at least asked, rather than informed me!"

"I thought it would be a pleasant evening for you—I thought you would enjoy it!" said Esther with a laugh. "I never thought it would be such a problem!"

Indeed, she could tell the rest of the Fitzroy family thought she was quite of her mind.

The fire was lit in the grate and candles were dotted about the drawing room, dinner having finished a little while earlier. Sophia was in the large armchair by the fire, watching the crackling fire, and their Papa was smoking his pipe in the opposing chair. Selina was seated by the window in Sophia's usual seat.

They had not heard from Arabella in some time, likely as not too busy enjoying the delights that a Christmas in Bath could offer. Esther could well remember, years ago now, how much she had enjoyed her time there. Lucy had accompanied her, and they had both enjoyed themselves splendidly.

It was part of the reason why Esther had been so certain Lucy would agree to her plan for this evening. But for some reason, it had not been welcomed in the slightest.

"Papa, tell her I do not have to go," said Lucy with a heavy sigh, standing by the door. "I have no wish to go!"

"If you have no wish to go," started their Papa calmly.

"But I have already purchased four tickets, and Sophia is too young to come—sorry, Sophia," Esther added hastily.

"Well, that is your fault," Lucy snapped. "Not everyone wants to be gallivanting off all the time, though I seem to recall you used to be perfectly happy with an evening at home!"

Esther gaped at her sister. Well, there was something rather strange going on here, and no mistake. *Since when did Lucy enjoy staying at home?* They all loved their parents, of course, but that did not mean they were willing to wait around to be entertained.

Why, last Christmas they had not seen hide nor hair of Lucy for three days when a traveling troupe of musicians had come into town!

"And I do not even like opera—not that much, anyway."

Esther frowned, and Lucy had the good grace to look sheepish.

"Not as much as you, anyway," she conceded. "Why you thought the opera would be a suitable evening for us—"

"For all of you," interrupted their mother.

Lucy spun around. "What do you mean?"

Esther sighed, stroking her silk skirts. She had dressed for the opera immediately after dinner and had come downstairs to find Lucy had made no move to dress for the opera at all. Why, she was still there in her cotton muslin!

She was beginning to seriously wonder whether she had made a grave error. Should she perhaps have asked Lucy, rather than merely inform her?

But there had not been time. Her eagerness to see Jack again was making it almost impossible to think clearly. That would explain why she chose to purchase four tickets for that very evening.

"Well, did not Esther say she had four tickets?" said Selina mildly. "I would have thought that meant there were four of you going."

Lucy turned to Esther with a sharp look. "If you have invited two dull gentlemen—"

"That is no way to speak to your sister," came the sharp reproof of their father.

Esther tried not to look hurt.

"I apologize," said Lucy stiffly, none of the fire leaving her eyes. "But I have no wish to spend the evening with dullards who cannot string a sentence together and think the height of humor is—"

"I will be accompanied by the Duke of Kendal," Esther said quietly, hoping their parents did not hear.

Lucy's eyebrows rose. "But you hardly know him!"

"And," persevered Esther, certain she would win over her sister if allowed to get a word in edgeways, "I invited Percy. He has accepted—he will be there soon, waiting for us."

In an instant, all the clouds lifted from Lucy's brow. A wide smile danced across her lips, and her shoulders relaxed. "Well, why on earth did you not say so?" she said as though she had never shouted at her sister in her life. "Wait for me to change, won't you?"

She had scampered out of the room without waiting for a reply—which was just as well, for Esther was not sure she could have given one.

Sighing heavily, she sat on the end of the sofa.

"You should have started with that," said Sophia with a wry smile.

Esther had to laugh. "Yes, I suppose I should. I am sorry you are not coming, Soph, I did not think—"

"When I am officially out, you may invite me all over town, but not before," her youngest sister said with a wry laugh. "Do not worry yourself, I shall be perfectly content here."

"Yes, after all," chimed in their Papa, "she has the better

company."

Laughter rang out around the drawing room as Lucy hurtled back into the room. "What are you laughing at? Are you ready, Esther, we don't want to keep Percy waiting. Are we taking the carriage? Is that what you're wearing?"

It was on the tip of her tongue to say acerbically that as it was her treat, Esther had no requirement to explain anything—but it would be preferable to have it all out now, rather than endure a constant barrage of questions on the way there.

And the sooner they left, Esther told herself, *the sooner she would see him.* Jack.

"We're laughing at Papa. I am ready, we are taking the carriage, this is what I'm wearing," said Esther in a rush. "What's wrong with it?"

She looked at the silk gown she had chosen for this evening. True, it was a cast off from Jemima, and that meant the jade green silk was a little brash against her hair—but she thought it was rather striking.

Now, with her sister's words ringing in her ears, Esther was not sure. After all, this was her first opportunity to really dress up for Jack—*not for him,* she reminded herself. *For the opera.* Jack just happened to be there.

"I do not know, you just look...different," said Lucy, pulling on her gloves.

A strange twist in the pit of Esther's stomach churned horribly. "Good different?"

"Just different," shrugged her sister most unhelpfully. "Come on, we'll be late!"

Rolling her eyes at her sister's frustrating ability to turn a situation around, Esther smiled at her parents. "We will not be back too late."

"Wrap up warm," warned her Papa. "'Tis mighty cold out there. I would hate for you to catch a chill this close to Christmas!"

"Who did you say you were going with?" asked her Mama.

Esther hesitated. She had not really liked saying his name, even his title, before her family—but there was no point in hiding it, Lucy would be spending the evening with them before long.

"The Duke of Kendal."

"What about old Kendal?" asked Caroline, striding into the drawing room and scattering snow all over the place. "Mercy, it's unpleasant out there. You look pretty, Esther."

Esther could not help but beam. It had just been the two of them with their mother for a little while—a very little while, she could barely remember it—but it was pleasant to have one's efforts for one's attire noticed.

"Thank you," she said warmly.

"Caroline, you're getting snow all over the carpet!"

"What did you say about Kendal?" Caroline repeated, ignoring her mother.

Esther swallowed. She certainly would not have said anything if she had known Caroline was coming to visit—but there was nothing for it now.

"Esther and Lucy are going to the opera with Percy and the Duke of Kendal," came Sophia's voice from near the fire.

Esther tried to give her sister a warning look, though it was too late.

Caroline's eyes widened as she shook her shoulders, letting the remnants of snow in her hair fall. "The Duke of Kendal? You and him, attending the opera together?"

"With Lucy and Percy," Esther added hastily, though that did more damage than good.

"What, as chaperones?"

"No," said Esther firmly, refusing to meet Caroline's eye.

"Damnit, Esther, we could probably do with a chaperone."

Well, it was not entirely a lie. Really, one could argue that she and Jack were acting as chaperones for Lucy and Percy. Esther almost smiled at that, the idea was so ridiculous.

"Are...well, are you sure that," Caroline began, concern creasing her forehead.

The door flew open. "I thought you wanted to go to this opera!" Lucy said, bundled up in a pelisse, fur, and bonnet. "Come on!"

Relieved to have an excuse to leave the conversation, Esther stepped forward. "Yes, Lucy, I am coming—do not concern yourself Caroline, everything is under control, and we will certainly wrap up warm, Papa. Do not wait up, Mama, we will be late."

She closed the door before anyone else in her family could question her about that evening and took a deep breath.

Everything under control. She barely felt under control herself. How was she supposed to attend the opera, in public, with all these thoughts and emotions churning within her? Esther had believed it a suitable place to sit and talk and perhaps steal a kiss...but now she was starting to wonder. Was it a little too public?

"If you do not hurry up, we shall be late," said a stern Lucy, who suddenly seemed very interested in attending the opera.

"Yes, yes," murmured Esther as she pulled on a pelisse, choosing a fur stole at random to throw over her shoulders, and wondering if she had enough time to find her gloves.

"Come on!"

The carriage was waiting for them outside; Esther had had the good sense to gain her father's blessing in the early afternoon to ensure it would be ready for them.

"Are we picking up Percy on the way?" asked Lucy as she clambered into the carriage. "Goodness, it's perishing in here!"

"No, we will meet both of them at the opera house," Esther replied as she got in. "Drive on!"

There were few places in the center of London that were far. Indeed, if it had not been such an inclement December, Esther would have suggested they walk, get a little fresh air.

As it was, they were descending from the carriage within twenty minutes, the street absolutely packed with other coaches, barouches, shouts and screams of delight, gentlemen hallooing each other, and ladies fluttering their fans, and it was only by very good luck that Esther was able to prevent Lucy from stepping into some rather fresh-looking horse droppings.

"Where are they?" Lucy said, eagerly looking round. "Did you suggest—"

Phhooeee!

A whistle rang out across the street, one that Esther knew only too well.

Both the Fitzroy sisters looked in the direction of the call and saw a beaming Percy, leaning against the opera wall.

"There he is!" Lucy said happily, pushing through the crowd. "Hie there, Percy, did you ever think this morning we'd be attending the opera tonight!"

Esther could not help but smile as she watched her sister warmly greeted by their friend. Well, she had known inviting Percy to accompany them was a good idea. It was strange though, standing here alone. There was no sign of Jack, as far as she could see, and it was odd to be so separate from Lucy and Percy, all the way over—

Esther gasped. Someone, and she had a very good idea who, had just delicately kissed her neck, the smallest part of which was exposed to the December air.

Jack stepped round her with a grin as Esther flushed. Oh, there was no point in attempting to deny it to herself. She was not just in danger of falling in love with the Duke of Kendal; in a way, she already was.

There was no one else she would ever permit to do that to her; no one else she wanted to do that to her. Only one gentleman in the world who she wanted kissing her neck.

"Ready?"

Esther swallowed. Whatever she was letting herself in for, she was certainly not ready. But she nodded, all the same. How could she deny him?

They met with Lucy and Percy by the large double doors into the opera house.

"This is Percy," Lucy said impulsively.

Esther flushed. That was certainly not how one introduced someone to a duke!

But it appeared that Jack did not mind. "Jack," he said, bowing to their friend. "I have heard much about you."

"Goodness, I haven't heard anything about you at all," said Percy with a grin. "Have you known the family long?"

"About three weeks," said Jack cheerfully. "I was introduced by Cheshire."

"Cheshire?"

Esther watched the confusion spread across Percy's face as the four of them ascended the stairs to the box she had purchased, then understanding dawned.

"Oh, you mean Walsingham!" said Percy with a grin. "I forget sometimes he's managed to snag a fancy title, rather impressive though I say so myself. I am only a lord."

"And I am the Duke of Kendal," said Jack smoothly. "But who's counting?"

The two gentlemen laughed as they reached the box, and Esther realized with a flush of delight that this was precisely what she had wanted. Not just a gentleman who could pleasure her, who teased her and made her laugh—but a man who melded with her family. Percy was almost family, after all.

"Esther?"

Esther blinked. Her sister, Percy, and Jack were all staring at her. "I beg your pardon?"

Jack smiled, and Esther could not help but shiver. This was a mistake. She should never have invited Percy and Lucy. A foolish error. She would never be able to restrain herself before them, and they would immediately know she was falling head over heels in love with the Duke of Kendal.

"Are you ready to go in?" asked Jack. "I had not realized you had purchased an entire box."

Esther tried to shake herself back into the moment. The noise of the gathering crowds beyond the box was growing, and it would surely not be long before the performance began.

"Yes—yes, of course," she said with a smile. "In we go."

She had only been in a box once before and that had been in Bath. Esther was astonished to find this one more extravagant than she remembered. This was all red velvet and gold. Gold brocade around the chairs, gold gilt around the chandelier above them, every inch luxurious.

"How on earth did you afford this?" asked Jack quietly as Esther sat at the end of the row.

Esther smiled weakly. "Easily, I am afraid."

For a moment, she thought she had given herself away, but Jack did not seem to notice. He was too busy watching her sister and Percy settle at the other end of the short row. Two seats lay between them.

"How long until the wedding?"

Esther's jaw dropped. *No. Surely not—surely that was not the way Jack intended to propose!*

Mouth dry, utterly unable to believe he had said such a thing, Esther tried to form the words to ask a question, but it was not within her reach.

"I would have thought soon, by the look of them," said Jack with a wry smile.

Esther closed her mouth and frowned. *Them? Not themselves, then. What on earth was he talking about?*

Percy said something indistinct, and Lucy roared with laughter.

Esther's face relaxed. "Oh, you mean—they are not engaged to be married," she corrected Jack with a laugh. "Goodness, the very idea!"

But for some reason, Jack was not laughing. In fact, he was frowning. "Are you sure? I would have thought—"

Whatever it was he thought, Esther was never to discover. Music, loud and passionate, suddenly burst out through the opera house, and they joined in the polite applause to welcome the performers onstage.

She really thought she would enjoy the opera; she was not musical herself, nor were most of her sisters, but their Fitzroy cousin Harmony was particularly talented. Esther had always greatly enjoyed her playing.

Yet that did not matter. Esther found her attention wholly focused on the gentleman beside her, the warmth of him, the sense of him, his proximity.

The first scene was not yet over when Jack carefully took her hand in his.

"I did promise," he breathed in her ear, "that I would hold your hand."

Esther shivered with anticipation, though he had done nothing yet to warrant such a response. Was he that bold? Would he even consider touching her, stroking her, teasing her in such a public place as this?

"We really should enjoy the opera," she breathed, trying not to take her eyes from the stage, on which a woman bemoaned in her best Italian just how unfair the world was. "It is has been acclaimed as—"

"Opera be damned," Jack said, cutting across her with a murmur. "I did not come to see the opera. I came to see you."

Unable to help herself, Esther turned and almost kissed him, Jack was that close.

"We shouldn't," she breathed, seeing the gleam of mischief and desire in his eyes.

Oh, he was bold. The Duke of Kendal may have little fortune left, but his nerve had never left him, and if Esther was not very much mistaken—

"We shouldn't," Jack said in a low voice, his hand releasing her own. "But we will."

Esther gasped and arched her back in the velvet opera seat as Jack's hand came to rest between her legs, its heavy weight against her secret place already building an ache in her.

Oh, she shouldn't—she should not let him. It was most disgraceful to even think such a thing, and yet…and yet…

"Jack," Esther breathed, unable to say any more. "Jack…"

It was not exactly a whimper, but not far from it. Jack breathed out slowly, heavily, saying nothing, not even looking at her anymore, but in the darkness of the opera house, Esther felt his fingers brush against her.

Esther shifted slightly, lowering herself in the seat, her legs unconsciously spreading. *Oh, how she wanted him there, wanted him more, heavier, deeper…*

"Tell me, Esther," Jack breathed, only just enough for her to hear him. "Are you enjoying it?"

His finger curled in that instant, stroking against her, and Esther moaned, just slightly, trying to push her buttocks forward to feel more of him.

Oh, if he knew what he was doing to her…but he most know, mustn't he? Why else would Jack be doing this?

"I…I cannot concentrate…" Esther managed to say.

And then it was over. His hand was gone, returned to his lap, and Esther wanted to cry out in agonized frustration. How could he do that, start to build something in her that was so delightful, so sweet, just to take his fingers away before they had finished their work?

Before they had brought her to completion?

"I cannot concentrate either," said Jack in a low voice. "Let's get out of here."

Esther stared into his dark gray eyes, saw desire in them, and felt herself lean toward him. But no, she could not lose control here, not now. Not with Lucy and Percy just a few feet from them.

"We can't."

Jack's smile disappeared, a more serious expression overtaking his face, his gaze drifting to her breasts, then her lips, then back to her eyes. "Why not?"

CHAPTER EIGHT

THE NIGHT SKY of London appeared different, somehow.

Esther was not sure she could put into words how or why or what made her think the stars a little brighter, the night air a little crisper. Perhaps it was the rebellious walk they were on. She and Jack. The Duke of Kendal, a gentleman she did not know a month ago.

She shivered, the fur stole around her shoulders not enough to keep out the wintery chill. It was almost Christmas, only a week away, and the weather had followed suit, promising snow with every turn of its breeze.

This London did not appear to be her London. Esther could not recall the last time she had walked the streets at this time of night, if at all. The typical sorts of people she saw were gone, replaced by laughing gaggles of men on street corners, pie sellers, and people selling wares Esther could not quite make out.

There seemed to be a frisson in the air, one she did not understand, but filled her and fueled her to do something she had not planned but now seemed the most natural thing in the world.

Reaching out, she took Jack's hand. His fingers were cold; he was not wearing gloves. Neither was she.

Esther shivered at the unexpected intimacy as they meandered slowly down a street, no thought—at least in her mind—to where they were going.

They were just walking. The two of them, a Miss Fitzroy and the Duke of Kendal, two people who ordinarily should certainly not have much to do with each other. And yet tonight…

"Let's get out of here."

Esther swallowed and glanced up at Jack, who was looking ahead, no care in the world. What did she think she was doing? Going for a nighttime stroll with a gentleman, even one as noble and dignified as Jack, the Duke of Kendal, was invitation for scandal.

Good women of polite Society did not go for nighttime strolls with gentlemen! Certainly not with gentlemen who could do such things with his fingers…

A shiver rushed down her spine, and Esther wondered whether Jack had felt it, but he did not look at her. Then he squeezed her hand, and a rush of affection for him cascaded through Esther's heart.

If there was going to be a man she would risk her reputation for, it would be him. He offered all the exciting promise of the night, with all the respectability and notoriety of a duke.

If there was going to be anyone in the scandal sheets tomorrow, it would be her.

Esther tried to push the thought away, tried to tell herself that she was being dramatic. *Who was she—no one!* No one in Society would be that interested in a young miss walking with a gentleman, alone.

Except…except he was the Duke of Kendal. And she was now the Countess of Cheshire's sister.

Just as Esther was overcome with the absolute certainty that they should return to the opera, pretend they merely stepped outside for a breath of fresh air then returned, Jack spoke.

"You are having second thoughts."

"No I'm not!" Esther blurted out, before smiling ruefully. "Well. Perhaps. This is…well, not something I have done before."

"Nor I," said Jack in a quiet voice.

Esther raised an eyebrow. It was not that she disbelieved him as a matter of course, but it was hard to swallow that a gentleman such as him, in his position, had never taken a lady on a walk of this nature. Even if he was penniless.

"You do not believe me?" said Jack with a brief laugh. "I am heartbroken, Esther. I would have thought I had gained a little of your trust over the last few weeks."

"You have! It's not that I don't—you know what I mean," said Esther hastily.

Oh, why did her words always get so tangled when she looked at him? When her gaze met Jack's, it was impossible to think clearly, her lungs tight, her stomach lurching, parts of her tingling that certainly should not be…

"I simply meant you are more…more worldly wise than I am," Esther said, attempting to explain in a way that did not make her look a complete fool. "I mean, you are a duke!"

Jack snorted as they turned a corner. "So is that supposed to mean I have taken advantage of plenty of ladies?"

"Have you?"

Esther had not intended for the words to slip out, but there they were in the night air. They were not thankfully close enough to anyone else to hear her words, so only Jack saw the flush undoubtedly creeping across her face.

Why had she said such a thing? It was none of her concern, surely, whether Jack had gone on walks with young ladies before. Had kissed them. Had touched them as he touched her…

Jack halted and turned to look at her. "Esther, what is it you really wish to ask me?"

Esther swallowed. It was a rather unnerving habit of Jack's—the ability to see through her mumbled words, her attempts at clarity, and recognize she had a far greater question on her heart.

And if she truly wished for him to love her, love her as she now knew she loved him, was it not better to be open? To be honest? To reveal her heart, just as fragile and delicate as any other?

Taking a deep breath, Esther said quietly, "I just…this is all wonderful, Jack, what we are sharing, what you do to me when you…when you…"

"Touch you."

Flames licked at the corners of Esther's heart, but that was no longer the only thing throbbing.

"Yes," she breathed, looking into Jack's eyes. "But I cannot help but wonder…there must have been others."

It was not precisely a question, true, but Esther thought she should be congratulated for the way she managed to speak it out. At least she had managed to get halfway there, and she could see by the shifting storm clouds in Jack's gray eyes that she had been understood.

The few seconds between her words being uttered and his reply were agonizing.

"I am not going to lie to you," Jack said quietly, his gaze not leaving hers. "There have been others, but not in the way you imagine."

Esther frowned. "I think…I would like a little more detail than that."

A wry smile crept across Jack's face. "I thought you might. Well, here it is. I have never been in love before, never seen much need for it. When I have had needs, I have…well, when one is hungry, one eats. When one is thirsty, one drinks. And when one has a certain need…"

Esther swallowed, her gaze dropping to the pavement. *Yes, she understood.* He had paid for lovemaking, sourcing it from one of the courtesans roaming the streets of London.

"I see," she said dully.

"No, I do not think you do," said Jack softly, lifting up her chin with his hand so she was forced to look at his face. "Esther, neither of them meant anything to me. Not like…not like you."

Esther stared, his previous words sinking into her mind, chiming like a bell.

"I have never been in love before…"

What did that mean? Did that…did that mean that he was in

love now?

Her heart soared, joy rushed through her like a crashing wave, and in that moment, Esther wondered how she was still able to stand.

He loved her. Jack loved her.

True, he had not precisely said as much, but he had not needed to. Esther had known what he meant, what he had been trying to say, even if he had not quite had the words.

She understood him. They loved each other; whatever was past was not important, not anymore. Not now they had an understanding with each other.

"So," Jack said quietly, squeezing her hand and continuing to walk, Esther not putting up any resistance, not now her heart was soaring, "what did you think of the opera?"

Esther laughed, all the tension which had built in her lungs suddenly escaping, relief that she had finally found the gentleman she cared for exploding out of her.

"If I am perfectly honest," she said, beaming, "I did not pay much attention to the opera. I must apologize."

"Oh, I do not believe it is your fault," Jack said lightly, visible mischief dancing in his eyes, even in the darkness of the evening. "I suppose you had a slight distraction."

A slight distraction. Well, if that was what he wanted to call it, though as far as Esther could see, there was nothing slight about the way he touched her… the way he teased her… the way he made it impossible for her to concentrate. Yes, it was a shame they could not be engaged in such a thing now…

Esther looked surreptitiously around them, then glanced at a wall just to their left. What she would give to be pushed up against that, with Jack's lips on her and his fingers—

"I suppose you will have to make some sort of excuse."

Esther blinked. "What?"

"To your sister and her gentlemen friend," said Jack lightly. "For abandoning them."

"Oh, I do not think they will overly mind, if they notice at all," Esther shrugged.

That was the thing with Lucy, one of the things she had always admired about her sister. She was always absorbed in what she was doing, no distracting daydreams for her.

"And I suppose I should apologize, too."

"What, to Lucy?"

Jack shook his head as they turned a corner onto a much quieter street. "No, to you."

It was a most unexpected thing for any gentleman to say, let alone one who was walking hand in hand with her.

Esther stared. "To me? What on earth for?"

She felt as well as heard Jack's chuckle, his hand shifting in hers, and it did something strange to her stomach she could not explain.

"Esther Fitzroy, this was hardly the courting evening I had intended," Jack said softly.

Esther glanced up at him, her stomach turning over. "You are? Courting me, I mean?"

His smile was broad. "Dear me, I am not doing a particularly impressive job of it if you have not noticed!"

A blush seared Esther's cheeks, and she looked at her feet as they continued down the dark quiet street.

He was courting her; well, she had known that from their very first walk, had she not?

She had known, even then, that Jack, Duke of Kendal, was interested in her—but her dowry, not her person. *At least, not her personality*, Esther corrected, heart soaring.

And she had been determined then, had she not, that she would tempt him, tease him, make him care for her.

"I have never been in love before…"

Esther's heart fluttered with excitement as the knowledge that Jack cared for her soared through her. He loved her. Even if he had not said the words, was that not what he meant? Was that not what he had hinted at, his reserve holding him back just a little, even now?

Still, a dark part of her mind whispered, *she did not know for certain.* The words had not been spoken.

Until then, how could she really be sure?

"Have you ever courted anyone before?" Esther asked, as lightly as she could, even if her heart was thumping most uncomfortably. "Before me, I mean?"

Jack's smile was a little too knowing for her liking. "Why? Would you take against me if I had?"

"No!"

"Good," he replied with a laugh. "For I have had little example set for me, and try as I might, it has been difficult to...to untangle my feelings for you, Esther."

There was a strange look on the duke's face as he spoke; Esther could see it in the darkness. Something he had been holding back but seemed to be slowly releasing.

"Little example? Your parents were...were not affectionate to each other?"

The laugh that emanated from his lips was dry, bitter, with no mirth at all. "Affectionate? I do not believe they knew the meaning of the word. There was certainly desire, yes, but for riches, for status, for the privilege granted them by their titles. No, I would describe neither of my parents as affectionate."

Such sadness dripped from each word that Esther found herself unable to bear the misery in his tone.

Jack was lonely. Here was a man who clearly had little care or fondness in his childhood, and perhaps none now; he was the duke, after all, so his father was gone.

"That is...awful."

"You think so?"

Esther nodded. "Every child, every person should know they are loved."

"But if they are not?"

It was not something she had ever had to wrestle with before. Every child in the Fitzroy family had been beloved, even those who had different parents. Esther had never been in any doubt of her place in the world and the people who cared for her.

But Jack…

He'd had, by the sound of it, a very different experience. One Esther would not have wished on anyone.

"In some ways," Jack said quietly, "I do not really know what love looks like. At least…I did not. Until I met you."

Esther did not know precisely what made her do it. There was no earthly reason why she should and a myriad of reasons why she should not. That did not matter. She did it anyway.

Halting and twisting into his arms, Esther kissed Jack fiercely, as though she could wipe away all the hurt in his past and all the frustration they had built together in one kiss.

The passion of her ardor was instantly matched by that of his own. Jack did not hesitate in pushing her up against the wall they had been walking beside, desire flowing through them like static, charging up one as the other gasped for breath.

Esther was not entirely sure what was happening, her senses unable to cope with such innumerable things happening.

Jack's lips on hers, his fingers in her hair, another hand on her buttocks, cradling her forward, the sense of his chest pressed up against her breasts, his manhood hard and desperate and pushing into her hip—

And it was more, more than that, for each of these merely built the ache within her, an ache Esther was now starting to crave. It grew deeper, more fiery, as Jack's tongue caught hers and tangled it in a wash of pleasure and desire, and Esther moaned in his mouth, unable to help herself.

"Esther—"

"Jack," she breathed, pulling him back into her arms.

By God, she wanted him—him and nothing else, the rest of the world be damned. The opera house, Lucy, Percy, the people they had passed on the street—all were forgotten as Esther lost herself in the overflow of sensation.

Somehow her leg was lifted, Jack's hand burning her thigh as he brought it around his hip, and Esther gasped at the intensity of it, the feeling they were closer, more tightly wrapped together, than—

"Now then! Not here, if you don't mind, miss."

Startled, heart pounding, Esther stared at a man on the other side of the street.

Jack slowly lowered her leg and whispered, "Leave this to me."

Esther was desperately trying to get her breath back, unable to speak and barely able to think. What did he mean, leave it to him? What was happening—who was that man?

"Stay here."

"Jack—"

"I said, stay here," Jack muttered in a growl that made her shiver.

She shivered slightly as she leaned against the wall, the warmth of Jack's embrace gone. The duke walked to the other side of the street and started to talk in a low voice to the man.

What was happening? Was it possible—and the thought made Esther's throat dry—that he recognized her? Was he about to go to her parents, reveal the scandalous behavior she was exhibiting on the street? To think, if the gossip sheets heard about this…

It was a torturous few minutes waiting, the murmurs from the men entirely unintelligible by the time they reached Esther's ears, but eventually the stranger nodded, muttered one last thing to Jack, and continued on his way.

Esther straightened up as Jack returned to her. "What did he want?"

There was a strange smile on the duke's face as he took her hand. "Nothing from you."

"But he wanted something," she insisted, remembering the way he had called out to them from across the street.

Jack sighed. "He…well. He thought you were a…a lady of the night."

A dark flush coated Esther's cheeks as the words rang in her mind. *A lady of the night?* He thought—that man had thought she was a courtesan!

"I hope you put him right," she said hotly, unsure how she was able to meet the Duke of Kendal's eye after hearing such words. *A lady of the night!*

Jack grinned, that look of mischief she adored appearing in his eye. "Nothing of the sort. I told him you were my paramour, and I had every intention of taking you to my rooms, but we had become a little…delayed, shall we say."

Esther stared. "You did what?"

"You wanted him to know you were a young lady, with a reputation to protect—a reputation to lose?" asked Jack.

She opened her mouth to argue and thought better of it. Well, perhaps it was a good thing Jack had managed to convince the man to go away. He was right; the last thing she needed was to flaunt her name and reputation here.

"Well, I am not sure how I am supposed to go home after that!"

Jack met her gaze. "Then don't."

CHAPTER NINE

ESTHER SWALLOWED, JACK'S words still ringing in her ears.

"Well, I am not sure how I am supposed to go home after that!"

"Then don't."

What on earth could he be talking about? There was nowhere else for her to go, no other friends or family in London she could simply turn up on their doorstep—not at this time of night, anyway.

Where did he think she should go?

"I…I do not understand," she confessed, feeling a little foolish at the admission.

Jack smiled. "Of course, I should have realized—you, Miss Esther Fitzroy, are far too innocent to know."

Too innocent to know. It was strange; Esther would have considered herself a relatively innocent woman in Society, it was true. At least, until a few weeks ago.

Now, knowing what they had shared, what he had done to her, how they had kissed…

Esther was not sure she could be described as innocent, not any longer.

But evidently there was far more to this type of world than she had initially thought. After all, Jack was still looking at her as though she had not quite worked out a secret yet, though how she was supposed to know without being told…

"There are…boarding houses, let us call them," said Jack delicately. "Places one can go—or I should say, two can go."

Esther stared. Perhaps it was the lack of light, the stars now hidden by growing clouds, but she could not comprehend him—yet embarrassment scalded her cheeks at the thought of asking for further clarification.

Somehow, and she did not know how, Esther felt as though she was on the edge of a precipice. As though she was right on the tipping point of entering a new world, a new understanding, one which was about to drop her into something entirely new.

Entirely forbidden.

"Boarding houses," she repeated in a quiet voice.

Jack nodded. "Rooms for the night, if you catch my drift."

Her mouth fell open. *Oh, yes, now she understood.* Rooms for the night. The sort of disgraceful behavior one was to expect from others, if they were so rebellious as to choose it.

But her? A Fitzroy?

Absolutely not. Esther had her sisters' reputations to think of, even if she were to ignore her own. How was someone like Lucy or Sophia to find a match if their sister was thrown out of polite Society for such wanton behavior?

Worse, how would Caroline hold her head up high at St James's Court if her sister was known to be a…a…

Esther did not even have the words to describe what she would be if she acquiesced to Jack's unspoken request. A light skirt?

Even that did not adequately summarize the state of entire wantonness!

"Rooms for the night, if you catch my drift."

She swallowed, trying to keep calm. He had not precisely suggested what she believed he was thinking, however, and she could not pretend the idea did not…well. Excite her. Entice her.

The thought of her and Jack, together, alone. Not propped up against a wall, a hallway, an alleyway. Able to enjoy each other, to slow down, not to rush the pleasure they sought.

To be in a bed...

"I should not have mentioned it."

Esther's gaze had drifted away but she looked at him as she spoke. "I did not say no."

How had she been able to say such words? She saw the impact of those words in Jack's expression—confusion at first, then shock, then desire.

He took a step closer to her, taking her hands in his own. "I do not suggest it lightly."

"I know," breathed Esther, unable to think now her hands were in his.

She was foolish to even attempt to convince herself. She was entirely his. There was no one else in the world she wished to be possessed by. The thought of what Jack could do to her, what they could share together, if they just had their own bed...

And no one would be expecting her home for a good while, would they? Operas ran long, everyone knew that. Lucy would assume she had gone home, likely to bed, and her family thought she was at the opera.

There would be no better time to...to make love.

"Esther," breathed Jack.

Esther smiled unconsciously as she saw the devotion in his eyes. He cared for her. Whether Jack knew it or not, he had fallen in love with her—and would certainly fall in love with her, she was certain, once they...consummated that love.

And it struck her, rather painfully, that in that moment Society and propriety, and her reputation...none of them mattered like he mattered.

She nodded, unable to speak, but knowing what she wanted. It was not a ring and a proposal, not precisely in the way she had hoped for, but no golden ring, no number of golden rings, could be as precious as what they were about to share.

As what Jack was about to show her.

"Are you sure?" asked Jack urgently under his breath. "Because I would not—I am not the sort of man to take advantage of a woman's indecision. You must be certain, Esther, certain that you want…that you want me."

And it was easy, hearing that, for Esther to smile. "I want you, Jack."

A smile broke over Jack's face, one so pure she knew he had been just as uncertain, just as nervous to secure her affection as she was his. Here they were, two people who loved each other—and would now dance over the line of propriety to experience that love.

"Come on then."

Before Esther could say a word, Jack had started walking rapidly, his feet pacing the pavement. With her hand in his, it was all she could do to keep up with him, her heart beating a rhythm that matched their footsteps.

She was really doing this. She was going to experience what only married couples usually shared.

Though Esther knew London well, Jack quickly led her to a district she did not know—and there was a reason for that. This was not one that respectable young ladies frequented or even visited.

Street signs passed in a blur, twists and turns taken so rapidly Esther did not know precisely where they were, and the streets started to fill up once more with people. But not the genteel people outside the opera house, laughing and jesting away.

Oh, no. These were the sort of people Esther had always been told to avoid: ruffians, thugs, women with their breasts almost out of their gowns, leaning in doorways and shouting invitations to passing men.

Esther bowed her head and wished to goodness she had thought to bring her bonnet, still lying by her seat in the opera house. It would have afforded her a little anonymity—or at least, it might have done. Perhaps its carefully embroidered peak and its sumptuous ribbons would have made her more of a target.

It was with great relief that Esther found her arm no longer tugged. Jack had stopped outside what appeared to be a hotel of some sort.

Though it was not of the typical milieu a Fitzroy would occasion, it did at least have a sign, and the windows were not boarded or broken.

Esther took a deep breath. "Is…is this…?"

"Say nothing when we enter," said Jack in a low voice. "Nothing."

She nodded. There was no time to speak; the duke had already opened the door and pulled her through, forcing the breath from her lungs—the breath she had only just managed to get back.

The lobby was dingy, but it was clean. At least, as far as Esther could tell. She had dropped her gaze and so found herself examining the floor—wooden, with a rug that had seen better days—as Jack's low voice muttered above her.

"Just the one night…one night…ah."

Esther looked up. Though she had not caught the conversation in full, there was a certain discomfort in Jack's voice she now knew well.

It appeared the issue of payment had occurred.

"Here," she murmured, handing him her reticule.

She could not precisely see the expression on Jack's face as he took it, but Esther found she did not want to. It would not be long, after all, until they were married, and he would never have to concern himself with money again.

Money having changed hands, Jack was handed a silver key by the woman at the desk. She smiled horribly at them, and Esther looked back at the floor with scalding cheeks.

Of course, she would not understand; she could not possibly know this was not a sordid assignation. This was love.

"Upstairs, take a left, third door on the right," said the woman curtly. "Have a pleasant…visit."

It was on the tip of Esther's tongue to say rudely that they would, but she was not given the chance. Jack had already started for the stairs, and with her hand still in his, she was pulled along.

Something was making an awful racket as they ascended to the next floor, and it was only when they started along the corridor, Jack counting doors under his breath, that Esther realized what it was.

Her heart. Her heart was thumping so loudly within her chest that it was quite impossible to hear anything else.

What was she doing? Could she really do this, go through with making love with the Duke of Kendal?

But as soon as Esther looked up into Jack's eyes, his face smiling and reassuring as always, she knew. The location may be disreputable, but their love was not. This was special, precious. Something they would treasure for the rest of their lives.

Jack opened the door and Esther gasped.

Although not entirely sure what she had expected, it was certainly not this. Opulent was not the right word; the bedchamber was rather more than that.

A thick, soft carpet lined the floor, with two rugs on either side of the huge four-poster bed that stood in the center of the room, luscious red velvet curtains hanging on each side. There was a dressing table, a set of chairs, a sofa, and a fire burning in the grate.

Red velvet curtains that matched the bed hangings were drawn to over the large windows, and a chandelier, candles ablazing, scattered light across the room.

"What the…" breathed Esther as she was pulled into the room.

The door snapped shut behind them, the key turning in the lock, but she could not think on that. This was certainly not what she could have imagined from the look of the place on the street!

"Do you like it?"

"Like it?" Esther said, turning on the spot to look at the sumptuous painting on the ceiling, all cherubs and angels, fruit falling in cascades from horns which matched the large ornate filigree fruit bowl on a side table. "How on earth did you…"

Her words trailed away as the answer appeared in her mind, causing heated embarrassment in her chest.

Of course. What had he said?

"There have been others, but not in the way you imagine."

He had brought other ladies here. Well, she should have expected that—though the idea rather tainted the luxury.

Jack smiled wryly. "I know precisely what you are thinking, and you could not be more wrong."

Esther laughed nervously. "I could not?"

He shook his head. "I have never brought anyone here, anyone at all. I was…recommended this place by a friend, should I ever have need of it. I found myself this evening in need of it."

"In that case," she said shyly, "I…I am excited to share this with you."

It was as though Jack had been waiting for her to say that, or something like it, to give him the permission to rush forward and pull her into his arms. Sensations more intense than anything Esther had ever known soared through her body, making it impossible to do anything but gasp into his mouth and accept his adorations.

Not that his kisses were particularly reverent. Oh, he desired her, Esther knew that—could taste it in his kisses, his tongue darting into her mouth with eager hunger that stirred something just as dark within her.

Fingers clutching at his lapels, Esther did not know what overtook her, but before she knew it, she had pulled off his coat, his waistcoat, and half his shirt before Jack broke the kiss.

"Damn, Esther," he breathed, "if I had known there was such desire underneath that gown—"

"I did not know it was there either," she said hurriedly, a nervous smile dancing on her lips. "It's…it's you. You do this to me."

Jack groaned as she pulled his shirt off, letting it fall to the floor. "And are you going to entirely undress me?"

Esther hesitated, heart pounding. She certainly wished to,

however outrageous that was. "Y-Yes."

Her voice only shook a little, but she was rewarded by the moan of satisfaction the slipped past Jack's lips, his eyelashes fluttering, before his gaze pierced hers.

"I am yours," he whispered. "Do what you will with me."

Esther could do nothing but reach out for him, desperate for his closeness—but she was also stirred by a growing desire within her to do precisely what she would never have permitted herself to do in any other situation.

But this was different, wasn't it. This was Jack, the man she cared for more than any other. A man who was attempting to seduce her and doing a marvelous job at it.

A man who was eager to marry her.

The thought spurred her on, fingers scrabbling down the soft strength of his chest, wiry hair leading to her destination. The buttons on his breeches were uncomplicated, and one, two, three, they were released, and the fabric fell to the floor.

Esther stared. My goodness…

Well, she had known in theory what she would find under there, but even still…it was far more than she had expected. Far more.

"Esther?"

She did not reply, at least in words. As Jack stood there, naked save for his boots and his breeches pooling around them, Esther slowly knelt on the carpet right before him, his erect manhood just before her eyes.

"Esther!"

She could not have known just what reaction she would receive, but her instincts had led her true. She had only taken the tip of his manhood into her mouth at first, eager to know what he tasted like, what he felt like within her lips, but the sudden and twitching reaction that seemed to rush through Jack told her just what she needed to know.

He liked it. And she was willing to do almost anything he liked.

Hesitantly at first, but growing with confidence with every moment, Esther sucked his manhood into her mouth, feeling the throb of his desire, hearing the groans in Jack's throat as he leaned his hands on her shoulders.

"God, yes," he moaned. "Esther, what are you—oh!"

Esther had lifted her hands to his hips to stabilize herself at first, to ensure she did not tip over, but it appeared the additional contact spurred on something within him, and she started to move, her body knowing what he wanted even if she did not, pulling his manhood into her mouth then letting it slowly leave, growing slick with every movement.

"Mmmmm," Esther moaned, unable to stop herself.

It was heady glory, this ability to give pleasure—and she was giving pleasure, she could feel it in every twitch and moan of the man standing before her.

How had she never experienced this before—and how would she ever stop giving it?

"Esther, Esther, stop!"

Esther allowed Jack's manhood to slip from her mouth as she looked up, concerned she had hurt him. "I am sorry."

"Please...please do not be sorry," Jack panted, his hands still on her shoulders as though she was the only thing holding him upright. "I just...I want to finish inside you."

Finish inside her? Esther did not have time to ask precisely what this meant; Jack had swiftly pulled her to her feet, wrenched off his boots and breeches, and half pushed, half thrown her onto the bed.

The sheets were soft and warm, but not nearly as welcoming as Jack's body as he moved to cover hers.

"Esther," he murmured, kissing her eagerly.

Esther lost herself in his kisses, barely unable to take in the fact that she had a naked man upon her on a bed, until—

"Jack!"

Jack halted moving up her skirts immediately, looking at her with concern. "If you don't want to continue—"

"I don't…I don't know what continuing means," Esther confessed.

Though her heart beat painfully, she knew she had to say it. The last thing she wanted was to look a fool before him.

Jack smiled, gently brushing away a curl that was resting on her cheek, her hair almost entirely fallen from her pins. "Let me show you."

There was not a moment of hesitation within her. Esther nodded, looking up into the eyes of the man she loved.

Jack pushed up her skirts at the front to reveal…well, everything. Esther tried not to think about it, but he did not seem particularly concerned. Quite to the contrary, his eyes had darkened, and a hungry smile appeared on his lips.

"Tell me if you want me to stop," he breathed, and then he moved.

Esther gasped. Stop? Why would she want this to stop, this intensity she felt throughout her whole body as his manhood entered her, slowly, carefully, yet filling her with every inch that entered her.

Stop?

"Don't stop," she breathed.

Jack chuckled and she felt the very movement within her. "You haven't seen anything yet."

And he was right. Esther gasped, arching her back and giving into the pleasure that started to radiate through her body as Jack started to build a rhythm within her, a rhythm that matched the twisting of her hips, her body once again taking over and delivering what it knew she wanted.

"Jack!" Esther gasped, her hands gripping his shoulders as though she would slip off the world if she did not. "Yes, yes, yes!"

The ecstasy happened quite suddenly, tipping Esther over the edge into splendorous, glorious pleasure that took her sight and made it impossible to breathe—all she could do was scream his name.

"Jack!"

"Esther!" With several heavy thrusts that stroked the ripples of pleasure even further through her, Jack collapsed onto the bed next to her.

Esther tried to breathe, tried to blink, tried to see, but it was several moments before any of her senses save that of touch returned.

When they did, she saw Jack lying beside her, a wry smile on his face. "Damn, Esther. I could never have imagined...I did not think..."

Esther smiled, her voice ragged. "I...I do not know...thank you."

"Thank you?" Jack raised an eyebrow. "You think you were the only one to receive pleasure?"

Her cheeks flared with heat, though it was rather a relief to know she had given as well as received. "Well. Good."

"Good indeed," growled the man she loved. "Now, when you are recovered, I have more to show you."

"More?"

"Oh, so much more."

CHAPTER TEN

WHEN ESTHER AWOKE, she did what she always did every morning—luxuriated in the sensation that she did not have to get up quite yet.

There was hardly a rigorous custom in the Fitzroy family for early rising, and that meant breakfast was considered in many ways an optional occurrence for the Fitzroy sisters. Esther rarely saw it, preferring to stay in bed, eyes shut, enjoying the quiet and relaxed sensation of merely being curled up in a blanket.

Which was why, when she finally opened her eyes, Esther was rather astonished to find that she was not curled up in a blanket.

She did not appear, even, to be home.

The room that swam into view, her eyelids still heavy with sleep, was far more grandiose than her bedchamber. The elegant paintings on the walls, framed in gold gilt, were not hers; neither was the bouquet of flowers carefully arranged in a vase on a console table she did not recognize.

Esther blinked. *What on earth...*

Then the memories of last night flooded back into her mind.

"Now, when you are recovered, I have more to show you."

"More?"

"Oh, so much more."

A strange sort of twisting in her stomach gave way to the

warm and heady sensation that she had done precisely what she had intended.

She had made Jack, the Duke of Kendal, fall in love with her.

"I have never been in love before…"

It was hard to believe, except she was literally sitting in the evidence. The soft bed, the comfortable pillow, the dazzling light attempting to pour through the red velvet curtains…

They were all evidence she had truly done what Esther had never believed she would.

She had made love. She had permitted herself to be bedded by a gentleman to whom she was not wed—or rather, she had bedded him.

A slow, wry smile crept across her face. Perhaps she was the one who had led Jack down the path of iniquity.

Hardly able to believe she was doing this, and holding her breath for a reason unbeknownst to her, Esther turned and looked at the gentleman lying beside her in bed.

He was not there.

Well, not precisely. Though she was still utterly nude and tucked up in the bed, the sheets to her neck, Jack was not in bed. He was almost completely dressed, only his coat lying on the floor. He was sitting on the edge of the bed, looking away from her toward the windows. And he was entirely silent.

For a heart stopping moment, Esther was almost certain she knew why he had said nothing—other than in fear of waking her, of course.

He regretted it.

There was no other explanation. Had he not said before that he had bedded other women—satisfying a need, she thought he had called it—and, evidently, she had not impressed in comparison.

What she had believed was the most incredible night, a moment between them that surpassed the entirety of the rest of her life, had been to Jack…a disappointment.

Shame burnt through her, and Esther swallowed, not knowing how to broach the subject. They had stayed here all night. *All night.*

Esther sat up in bed, the sheets falling below her breasts before her fingers scrabbled to bring them up again.

They had stayed here all night; her parents would be wondering where she got to, and Lucy would tell them that she had left with the Duke of Kendal. They would go to his rooms and not find them—either of them—there.

What would they think?

The sudden movement evidently disturbed Jack for he turned to look at her.

Esther gasped at the expression on his face. It was wretched. Truly miserable.

Heart-breaking nausea rising in her stomach, it was impossible not to despair at the misery she had inflicted upon him. The Duke of Kendal did not love her. If he had cared for her even a little, he would not have looked at her with such sadness, such regret.

Esther hated it. Hated she had done her best, her everything, to encourage the Duke of Kendal, her Jack, to fall in love with her. She was not a flirt by nature, yet she had done all she could to entice him…and had failed. Even handing over her innocence had not worked.

She should have known, Esther told herself bitterly. She should have known Jack had not fallen in love with her. Now she thought about it, had he ever actually spoken words of love to her?

"I have never been in love before…"

He had hinted at it, to be sure, but that was not the same thing. He had made no promises, no declarations…and now she would have to navigate her way back home—if she could find the way at all—and explain to her parents precisely where she had been last night.

Heat scalded her cheeks. If she could even find the words.

Esther's gaze, having fallen to the bed, returned to Jack's

eyes, and her heart broke for him as well as herself. He looked absolutely wretched.

Instinctively, without a second thought, she reached out for him—but he flinched away, out of her reach. She swallowed, allowing her hand to drop to her side.

Esther sighed heavily and tried to collect her thoughts. If she had not been so presumptuous to assume she could make the Duke of Kendal love her, she never would have found herself in this position.

In this scandalous position.

"I…well," said Esther quietly, the pain of seeing Jack flinch from her still echoing in her heart. "I did not think I was that bad."

Voicing her fear made it somehow worse.

Well, it was not as though she had much practice in the art of making love! She was not a vagabond harlot, allowing anyone to play with her, touch her, tease her. She was no gentleman, who could dalliance with any number of people without attracting the reprehensible ire of Society.

Jack laughed bitterly, still seated on the edge of the bed. "Bad? You are the absolute best—the best I have ever…"

His voice trailed away, and Esther found to her chagrin that his words caused hope to spark in her heart—hope she quickly doused.

Perhaps she could go to Chalcroft? The seat of the Fitzroys was outside Bath, in the countryside. She would never have to see anyone again if she did not wish to.

"I have something to confess."

Esther looked up. There was such desolation in Jack's words, she had found them hard to make out at first—but it was clear on his face that he felt he had wronged her. Done something terrible. There was guilt in his eyes, a searing guilt that caused a shiver to rush down her spine.

What on earth could come next? Would he admit he had never even liked her—that the kisses he had bestowed, hot, frantic kisses she had reveled in, were false? Was it possible for a man to lie like that? Esther did not know, her total experience with gentleman solely the man sitting before her.

Jack sighed, turning to face her. "Miss Fitzroy, I—what?"

Esther smiled weakly. "Goodness, it feels like the end of the world when you call me Miss Fitzroy."

"It is your name," he pointed out.

"Yet you have called me Esther almost our entire acquaintance," she said, not wanting to think about how short that time had been.

Had she perhaps rushed into this? Been so arrogant to think she could make Jack care for her, fall in love with her, that she did not consider how brief their acquaintance had been?

But had not Jemima agreed to marry Hugh within weeks of meeting him?

"True," said Jack with a heavy sigh. "But I felt at greater liberty to speak your name then. I cannot, in all conscience, do so now."

Esther swallowed, and for the first time wished she'd had enough presence of mind to put some clothes on before this conversation. The last thing she wanted, as Jack confessed to have no feelings for her, was to sit her entirely nude.

"So, Miss Fitzroy, I must confess," Jack said, his gaze meeting hers then dropping to his hands. "I...I have nothing to my name. Nothing at all."

For a heartbeat, Esther waited for the confession, but then realized he must mean his poverty—the poverty he did not know she was already aware of.

"Why, only yesterday he was telling me about the poor Duke of Kendal!"

It was difficult not to smile. If that was the only problem— why, was she not rich enough for the both of them? Would it not be easy to solve his money worries with her dowry?

"It would not be possible for me to purchase one single gold ring," said Jack ruefully, "let alone five."

Five—five gold rings?

For a moment, Esther was not entirely sure what he meant. What could the Duke of Kendal do with five gold rings?

Then she remembered their shared walk at the Christmas market, the five gold rings she had purchased for her sisters—then her stomach dropped.

Why would Jack want to buy her a gold ring? *Unless...unless he did care for her...*

"You do not need to apologize for your poverty," Esther said quietly, wishing desperately he would look up and meet her gaze. She did not make the mistake of reaching out for him again, certain he would retreat even further. "You think I measure a man by stocks and bonds?"

Jack's laugh was bitter. "You think that was my confession? Dear God, how I wish it was...no, my confession is even worse."

Esther's heart froze. *Worse? What could possibly be worse?*

Was he a bad man perhaps—a criminal? Had he actually lost his money in a nefarious manner, one which could not be countenanced? Was he not really a duke at all?

Her mind had no further time to guess at the wild speculation that rushed through her, for Jack took a deep breath, and spoke words with a heavy conscience.

"I...I decided to court you for your money, Esther, and that alone."

Esther swallowed. Well, she had worked that out for herself—she was hardly a fool; she had seen it in his eyes that first walk they had shared.

"I was wondering if you would like to go on another walk?"

He was not alone in his approach, though he had made the strongest impression.

"Of course," Jack said softly, "I never actually expected to bed you. That was never part of the plan."

A smile crept across Esther's lips. Here it was, the moment when Jack, the Duke of Kendal, admitted that it was also not in his plan to fall in love with her—but he did.

Silence eked out most uncomfortably.

It was only after a few more heartbeats that Esther realized, to her chagrin, that no further words were coming.

It was true then. Jack had not fallen in love with her. It was all over.

"I see," she said dully, pulling the sheets around herself as best she could, still highly conscious she was undressed. "So you never wish to see me again, now you have."

Jack shook his head. "Never see you again? I want to see you every single day for the rest of your life."

Stomach lurching, hardly able to believe what she was hearing, Esther could do nothing but stare at the gentleman who was not making any sense.

"I am, however, convinced you will never wish to see me again," Jack said wretchedly, his stormy gray eyes finally meeting hers. "Why would you wish to? I am a cad, a fool, a blaggard—I sought you because of your purse, not you personally. I am a wretch indeed, not worthy of you."

"But…" Esther could not understand.

He seemed to care for her—at least, he evidently felt awful for having pursued her merely for monetary gain. But was that because she had given him everything, everything she was when they had made love last night…or because he had fallen in love with her?

"Now, when you are recovered, I have more to show you."

"More?"

"Oh, so much more.

"I know your father will likely call me out when I return you home, and quite right too," Jack was saying. "I suppose if you had brothers—"

"But I do not want—Jack, I knew all along," Esther said hastily, realizing what he might think. *She was certainly not going to ask Hugh or Stuart to fight him!*

There was utter confusion on his face. "Knew?"

Esther nodded. Perhaps this was it, the reason they were at

such odds with each other; he thought his confession something diabolical, when in fact...

"It did not escape me that you were interested in seeing me because of my dowry," said Esther gently. "I am no fool, Jack. I have been in Society. I have met gentlemen before."

A look of shame and regret passed over Jack's face. "Ah."

"And I actually...well, my sister Caroline had already informed me of your...dire financial situation," said Esther, a little apologetically.

Well, it was rather awkward. How many other gentlemen's affairs did she know in that detail, after all? Not even her own brothers-in-laws'.

"So you see, I went into our...well, I do not think it is precisely what a courtship is, but whatever it is, I went in with my eyes wide open," said Esther quietly, hoping he could feel the heart within her words. "You did not deceive me."

For a few heart stopping moments, Jack merely sat, staring.

Then he laughed, shaking his head. "I should have known better than to underestimate the Fitzroy sisters."

"You should indeed," said Esther warmly, her heart lifting. *Did this mean...* "And when you think of it, Lucy and Sophia have the same dowry as me, you could have attached yourself to either of them. But you chose me."

It heartened her, this sudden realization. There were three Fitzroy sisters he could have pursued. But it had been her he had wanted.

Jack cleared his throat, looking uncomfortable again. Esther's heart sank. *Surely there could be no more to upset her?*

"Actually," Jack said awkwardly, "it was suggested to me that you might be the..."

"The easiest woman to win over?" Esther asked darkly.

"No!" Jack looked mortified at the very thought. "No, it was just...I was speaking with Cheshire about my need to marry a wealthy woman, and he suggested my heart would have to be in it, or else I could not follow through. I said he was wrong, and he told me he would prove it."

"Prove it?" Esther repeated.

This made no sense. Why on earth would her brother-in-law be saying such a thing—why would he...

"Cheshire said he had three sisters-in-law," said Jack darkly. "All wealthy, but the one I would truly care for—the one I was suited to—was you. He challenged me to woo you, to win your heart...and then see if mine could remain untouched."

"Cheshire said he had three sisters-in-law, all wealthy, but that the one I would truly care for—the one I was suited to—was you."

Esther stared, the words ringing in her ears...and then she finally understood.

Jack had been wooing her for her wealth, attempting not to lose his heart.

Esther had known she was being wooed for her wealth, determined to secure his heart.

And here they were, in a boarding house, having spent the night together entirely wantonly, each knowing they had fallen in love but not knowing that the other had too.

"You are laughing."

"Well, do you not think it is a little ridiculous?" Esther said, letting the sheet fall a little now, no longer worried about being exposed. *How could she be even more exposed with this man that she loved?* "Oh, Jack. I had promised myself to seduce you—well, at least to seduce your heart. And here you are, in love with me."

"And here you are," said Jack softly. "In love with me."

She smiled at him, unable to believe they had finally reached this level of happiness. Had anyone ever discovered this marvelous connection? Were they the first?

"Well, now that we understand each other," said Esther, "what do you want to do?"

A wry smile crept across Jack's face. "You will have to buy your own gold wedding ring, you know."

Esther's heart sang. She was going to marry him; she was going to be Jack's wife.

She was going to be the Duchess of Kendal.

That was a rather startling thought, but she pushed it aside for now. That could wait. All that mattered was that they loved each other, that they had found each other.

That they would be happy for a very long time.

"I will buy you five," she said in a teasing voice, "if you will marry me."

Jack leapt across the bed, pulling Esther into his arms—a place she moved to willingly. As their kiss sealed their agreement, she could not imagine being any happier than she was in this moment.

Well, not quite...

Esther pulled away, looking up into the devoted—and desirous—eyes of Jack, the Duke of Kendal. "There is one more thing you can do for me."

Jack arched an eyebrow. "And that is?"

It was impossible to even think of saying the words—at least, it had been, once. Now all that was changed. For the rest of her life, Esther would know precisely what she wanted, and how to ask for it.

"I want you," she said, just a little shyly, "to kiss me."

Jack leaned forward but Esther pulled back.

"Not there," breathed Esther, heart starting to beat frantically as the ache began building between her legs. "*There.*"

His eyes followed hers, and then they widened.

"Oh, Esther Fitzroy," Jack said with a grin, pulling down the bedsheet to reveal her body in all its glory, nestling himself between her legs and kissing her inner thigh. "Five gold rings are not good enough for you."

As his questing lips moved up her thigh to her secret place, warm and wet, twisting pleasure within her as his tongue darted in, Esther leaned back, her eyelashes fluttering.

Perhaps. But this would be a start.

About Emily E K Murdoch

If you love falling in love, then you've come to the right place.

I am a historian and writer and have a varied career to date: from examining medieval manuscripts to designing museum exhibitions, to working as a researcher for the BBC to working for the National Trust.

My books range from England 1050 to Texas 1848, and I can't wait for you to fall in love with my heroes and heroines!

Follow me on twitter and instagram @emilyekmurdoch, find me on facebook at facebook.com/theemilyekmurdoch, and read my blog at www.emilyekmurdoch.com.